Cybergasm

A Silly Tale of Holy War

Guida M. Jackson

To order additional copies of this book, contact:
Xlibris Corporation
1-888-795-4274
www.Xlibris.com
Orders@Xlibris.com
52106

For those repressed souls everywhere
who have ever fallen victim to the strictures of religious fervor

This story is inspired by a newspaper article in the early 2000s about a woman's campaign to remove a replica of Michelangelo's nude statue of David from a commercial building outside Houston because its exposed nether regions allegedly troubled her young son. Her campaign finally involved her entire evangelical church with the silly consequence that to keep peace the management attached a plaster fig leaf to the statue. In stormy weather this fig leaf tended to crumble and reveal portions of the dread member underneath, so constant vigil had to be maintained by the devoted mother for fear that her son might be traumatized by an unexpected revelation. This dedicated soul must have spent hours each day just looking up at that naked body, waiting for the slightest hint of infraction.

I have often thought about that poor woman's desperate plight, for I have never before known of a young child who was so offended by the sight of the human body. I have however known women—for I am one—who have been sufficiently indoctrinated by fundamentalism to be terrified of any hint of sexuality.

This story is not about that woman, whom I never knew; in fact, any similarity to anyone, living or dead, is coincidental. It is about all of us who go to great lengths to deny our own humanity, locking away our own repressed shadow self. It is about the caged animal, which is always dangerous.

1

These events occurred before the advent of sophisticated Spam filters

When the first message appeared on her office monitor, Vickie didn't interpret it as a threat and, given its lascivious nature and her own personal mortification, made the decision not to confide in anyone. It was the wrong decision.

It had seemed the logical one at the moment. The message was an insulting and vulgar insinuation spammed into her e-mail. That fact, taken alone, would indicate that it could have originated anywhere, and that she might be a random target:

Congratulations on your success making Michelangelo writhe in his grave. But woman, can you ignore that throbbing clit?

At first she didn't grasp its meaning, and, mired in the context of abbreviations for office terminology, she got out her manual and searched the index under the letter C. As she ran her finger down the Cl . . . Cli . . . Clit . . . , comprehension struck like a 220-volt charge. She slammed the book shut and hit the *Delete* key, casting right and left in her small cubicle to be sure no one could see.

The incident threatened to mar what had been her one small triumph for decency in Montgomery County. She had brought it about single-handedly, with the backing and at the instigation of her church. She had visited the shopping center manager every day for four months to complain about the vulgar statue of a naked man atop a cupola on the center's tallest building. To make it worse, the statue was supposed to depict David, a revered biblical king. The abomination was not only an affront to Christian sensibilities but also a sin. The manager's argument that all of the statuary were copies of famous works of art did not sway her, but her threat to stage a boycott by her entire enormous congregation apparently got his attention. He ordered the statue altered so that David was at least partially clothed. It just went to show what one small voice crying in the wilderness could accomplish.

The disturbing element about the offending message, and one she originally overlooked, was that it had appeared on her secured address, accessible only by special code available to no one outside her department. It was a small office, consisting of seven women and four men, besides the boss. She could easily figure which of the four wrote such a revolting suggestion. Only one, Teddy Caplock, used that kind of gutter language.

Obviously, she couldn't report it. How could she stand before Russ Winters' desk and repeat such an obscenity? Anyway, Mr. Winters wouldn't have taken her complaint seriously. Everyone knew better than to take Teddy seriously; even Teddy didn't take himself seriously.

Anyhow, she'd long ago learned how indispensable Winters considered Teddy to be. Once when she shared a crowded elevator with the two men, after a buxom woman stepped off, Teddy had elbowed his boss and said in a stage whisper loud enough to be heard by everyone, "Are those things real, or is she just carrying ballast for the extra load aft?" Winters had given an embarrassed chuckle and shot Vickie a boys-will-be-boys look. She was shocked.

Just before closing time, the second message appeared, this one not as overtly lewd. Yet for some reason, momentarily at least, she found it more disturbing than the first:

Unleash the craven beast within.

Before she could catch her breath, in seconds another appeared:

Unlock those thighs.

And then a third:

The caged animal is always dangerous.

Despite the vague intimation of menace, she deleted the messages and afforded them no more than a few minutes' disgust.

Second wrong decision.

The following day, when the next one appeared, she shook with outrage. She printed it, wishing she hadn't dismissed the first ones so lightly. Because theirs was a secured system solely for their department's use, deleted files were retrievable only by Gooch, the network administrator: a bearded sandaled nerd with a key to the executive restroom. She would never ask him to retrieve the messages, but obviously Gooch was falling down on the job. His spam detection software was supposed to prevent unwanted messages from penetrating the various departments' firewalls in the first place.

The new message was clearly beyond a joke, beyond even the poorest of taste. It was the work of Satan. Overcoming her natural modesty, she would take this one to Mr. Winters:

When will you let me DEVOUR you?

Strung tight with righteous indignation that overrode her reticence to display anything of a sexual nature to a man, she marched to the inner sanctum without knocking and tossed the message onto the startled Winters' desk. She couldn't prevent her voice from shaking. "This is the fifth piece of filth I've received in two days. Something's got to be done. I can't work under these conditions."

Her boss read the message with obvious irritation, his drawn sandy brows and plump puckered mouth plainly telegraphing his reaction: Why is this broad bothering me with this crap?

He almost said as much, as he flipped it back across the desk toward her. "A spammer that somehow got by Gooch. I'm sure he's on it by now. What do you expect me to do about it?"

"Clearly a spammer from inside this office who knows my code name. This is addressed to my code name. It doesn't take a genius to figure out who did it. I expect you to talk to him. Tell him this is a business office. Intra-office memos are supposed to be confined to course development, programming, and training. Nothing beyond that."

Winters sighed heavily, as if the weight of the giant corporation rested on his back, instead of merely one small department. He answered as if she were an errant child, except that he avoided looking at her, instead directing his gaze at the ceiling over her head. The bags under his eyes hung like pendulous breasts above the red-veined fleshiness of his cheeks.

"Supposing it did originate here. There are four men out there. What do you want me to do, accuse someone with no proof? What do you think that would do to morale if I were mistaken?"

He pushed away from his desk, a signal that she was dismissed. "Anyway, your indignation at the use of your e-mail for other than business is pretty hypocritical, considering the Obama cartoon you printed up and pinned over the coffee machine. Didn't you get that as an intra-office memo?"

She flushed and conceded defeat, but as she rose to leave, she thought of something else. With as much sarcasm as she dared, she said, "I believe you've overlooked someone. There are five."

"What's that?"

"Five men. Counting you."

She stalked back to her cubicle, taking the hated message with her. But although she relegated the original to the delete bin, she saved the hard copy, folding it squarely in two with trembling fingers and locking it in her bottom drawer.

By the sheerest force of self-discipline, she managed to put it out of her mind. But not before she'd imagined holding both Winters and Teddy Caplock by the hair and cracking their heads together.

Although she came in early the next morning, a new message was already waiting in her inbox. There it shone, crude and titillating, filling her small cubicle with seduction. She sucked in her breath in distaste, but printed it:

You know you want to spread 'em for me, babydoll.

Shaking, and with the tiniest tingle of excitement, she printed it before deleting it from her screen and deposited the hard copy in the desk. Sooner or later, if this kept up, Russ Winters was going to have to take action. But for now, for reasons not even clear to herself, she chose not to bring the matter to his attention again.

The wall clock read 9:02. She got up and went to the coffee bar, noting in passing that Teddy's cubicle was empty. On his desk was a framed photo of himself in ski garb hugging a toothy blonde, his dark well-moussed hair only slightly ruffled by the Aspen wind. Such a narcissist. She wondered if he had even known the blonde, or had only asked her to pose with him.

Sonja, one of the other women, was waiting beside the bar, freshly coiffed and painted, but looking glum and still sleep-stunned. "Coffee's not ready yet. It was Roberta's turn to make it, but she's always late. There ought to be some kind of penalty to the coffee person when they don't get here on time."

"Have you seen Teddy?" Vickie asked, trying to seem casual.

Sonja examined her with interest for a long second before she answered. "No more often than I can help. He won't be in this morning, thank God. Maybe we'll get some real work done without Mr. Hit-onsky. He had a dental appointment. Why can't he go on his day off like the rest of us?"

Vickie returned to her desk, determined from now on to check her e-mail the last thing before she left in the afternoon. She had neglected to note the time when the last message was sent. Probably Teddy had slipped one in just as he left the day before, knowing he wouldn't be in when she found it, and figuring that she would be puzzled. Or—worse thought—maybe he went home after work and sat around all evening fantasizing about her, composing lusty propositions to subdue his own unattainable desires.

Apparently, he had no real plans to act on his lewd suggestions. Just like the big blowhard. The whole thing was no more than an idle, hedonistic diversion to him.

Teddy kept a low profile once he returned to the office, and she presumed he'd had all the fun at her expense that he planned.

Or so she thought until the next message came.

It appeared on her screen on Friday afternoon, as she prepared to leave. The message was so vile that she had to make a copy:

You haven't lived until you have succumbed to asphyxiafilia. I promise the jolt of your life.

After she looked up the meaning of asphyxiafilia, Vickie's heart thumped like a tom tom. The creep had gone too far this time. No one, not even Russ Winters, could ignore this any longer. Maybe Teddy had lost it—maybe he was even dangerous. She had avoided him with great purpose all week long, so she could only guess at his frame of mind. He was hard to avoid, as a rule, forever leaning into someone's cubicle, bragging about a conquest to the men, trying to charm the women with crude jokes. How she wished for Aunt Jessie. She could have read him from across the room.

Strange that Jessie would come to mind.

But how Jessie would love Teddy. He was just her type. Jesse would know how to handle him.

It was her aunt, only eight years her senior, who introduced Vickie to the vulgar, tactile pleasures, the vulnerability of skin.

Jessie loved to dry off after a bath by standing in front of the rotating fan on the sun porch that served as an extra bedroom. The troubling fact was, access to the sun porch was only through Vickie's room, and as a girl she was often subjected to the sight of Jessie's nubile nakedness. On each occasion Jessie, who considered Vickie's parents far too strict, seized the opportunity to educate her.

As Jessie posed before the oscillating fan, Vickie once observed from the doorway, "If you're trying to get dry, you ought to fix the fan so it won't turn, so it'll blow on you all the time."

Her aunt came over and stooped down, bringing her scrubbed and shiny face close to Vickie's, her full breasts hanging like ripe fruit, the dark curls at the vee of her inner thighs glistening with beads of dampness.

"It's hard to explain, Victoria," Jessie said, growing serious. "The feeling of the breeze against your skin as it comes and then goes away, like a lover, then comes back again. It's tantalizing, seductive. You crave for it to hurry back. You'll understand better when you're older."

But although Vickie had filed this information in her mental archive, its meaning had thus far eluded her. Still, the memory persisted, beckoning her to a dark world that, in all her thirty-four years, she had never entered and never would, a world doubtless familiar to both Jessie and Teddy. Yes, nothing Teddy said would shock Jessie. Vickie could even picture them doing it.

Only in her daydream it wasn't Aunt Jessie at her current age of forty-two, but as she was back then at seventeen, all damp and glistening, just out of the bath and naked as a plucked chicken.

Teddy was another matter. She couldn't envision him in anything other than the slacks, sport coat and gaudy tie he consistently wore. Perhaps he would have unzipped his trousers just enough to remove the Part and insert it into Jessie so that it was safely out of view before Vickie's voyeuristic dream. She couldn't have borne seeing that actual disgusting Prod. Just thinking about it gave her the shuddering sweats, which meant her armpits would be sticky for the rest of the day.

Sticky. For the rest of the day.

She shook her head to clear it of the odious visitations by Satan and attempted to concentrate on something else, but . . . .

. . . Even when Teddy reined himself in at the office, she found him oddly disturbing. He might be discussing the project at hand in a businesslike manner, but she knew exactly what was really on his mind. And he was always around, underfoot like a piece of chewing gum, a reminder of things best forgotten.

This week, however, he had stayed close to his desk. Sonja confided that the dentist had pulled a tooth, and while Teddy waited for his bridgework, he wouldn't open his mouth in public.

Vickie put the latest offensive message away with the others, aware, belatedly, that everyone else had left for the day. Hurriedly she locked up her disks and rushed toward the elevator, tugging on her coat as she went.

Smoothing it fondly over her breasts.

Feeling their roundness beneath the soft wool.

The parking garage, inadequately lit by ancient buzzing and zapping fluorescent bulbs, was practically empty. As she made for the far end where her car was parked, the sound of footsteps behind her—heel taps—sent a prickly stab of alarm between her shoulder blades. The base of her head tingled.

Strange: no one had been on the elevator with her.

She paused and heard the heel taps stop and start up again when she resumed walking. They increased in speed as she, affecting nonchalance, lengthened her stride, not daring to walk faster—pride overriding even panic. She couldn't turn around to look, for fear it would be Teddy and then—

She had never been afraid of him before, but now he had proven himself more devious and despicable than she could have imagined. She couldn't begin to fathom such a warped and twisted mind as his must be. What did he want of her? It made her senses reel even to speculate.

A car whipped around the curve at the far end, coming from the level above. Its lights momentarily blinded her, but it veered well away from her as it sped past.

Hoping the lights would blind Teddy as well, she broke into a run, heading for her car at breathless speed, as if her very life were at stake.

2

As she gunned out of the garage that Friday afternoon, heart thumping against her breastbone, Vickie couldn't see in the rearview mirror who was following her, but she didn't need to see. No one else wore caps on his heels.

On the way home, she stopped by the church to share with the minister news of her shopping center triumph, but he had left for the day. She considered going by his house but decided not to take the chance that her visit would be misinterpreted. Her instincts warned her that the pastor had something of a crush on her. So she scratched a note telling him that the offending statue would soon be clothed. She left it on his desk, atop a folder labeled *Sermon Notes*. This would remind him to share her good news with the congregation on Sunday.

But the matter of Teddy quickly returned to mind. She fumed the entire weekend over his reprehensible conduct, then berated herself for allowing him to spoil her days off. She kept thinking that Aunt Jessie wouldn't have given the whole episode a second thought. Unless, perhaps, to feel flattered.

Repeatedly, Vickie choked back the notion. Wondered where it came from. Refused to think about Teddy or Aunt Jessie anymore.

Yet time and again, as she went about her mundane chores over the next two days, visions of Jessie rose from her memory. Like the time that her mother was collecting clothing for a church rummage sale, and Aunt Jessie had spied a black velvet dress among the lot. She pulled it out and said, "Ooh! Can I have this, Maudie?"

With a disapproving frown, Mama had said, "Why on earth? It's shabby and out of style; it's one Ned wore years ago for Eastern Star. Besides, it's much too large for you." Ned was Jessie's and Mama's oldest sister, a stern and commanding soul whom Vickie could easily imagine wearing the somber black dress.

"Good. Then no one would buy it anyway," Jessie said, and she breezed off with it before Mama could protest.

But later, when she and Vickie were alone, Jessie explained, dark eyes sparking with something akin to mischief, but not quite that. "Ned missed the whole point of having a plushy dress. You haven't lived until you've worn velvet wrong-side out next to your bare skin."

She picked up the dress from her daybed and thrust it at Vickie. "Go on. Try it. I don't mind."

Vickie felt herself flush and stammered, "Maybe later."

Jessie shrugged and proceeded to shuck her clothes with such quick abandon that Vickie had no chance to escape the performance. When Jessie was completely naked, she turned the dress inside out and slipped it over her head. As it slithered down her body, she closed her eyes and breathed an ecstatic, "Ahh!" She ran her hands up her thighs, over her breasts, down her shoulders, embracing herself, locking one leg around the other, her toes on the free foot splayed like a cat's.

She opened her eyes and addressed Vickie with great seriousness. "You don't know what you're missing, kid. You don't always have to have a man. This is like thousands of little silky fingers touching you all over."

For no reason, Jessie was still on Vickie's mind during the Sunday sermon and remained on her mind on Monday morning, while she strolled among the office cubicles, surreptitiously checking the men's shoes, even finding an excuse to consult with Mr. Winters so as to inspect his for heel caps. But his feet were hidden beneath his desk, and she could think of no legitimate reason to lure him out. She vowed to look at lunchtime, although she was sure he didn't wear taps. He wasn't the type.

Teddy, on the other hand, wore them on every pair of shoes he owned, not to preserve the heels of the expensive footwear, as he claimed, but to call attention to himself, she was certain. Everyone turned when he walked into a room—usually arriving late, to make a grand entrance. Whistling, sometimes, or jingling the coins in his pocket. Playing with himself, Sonja once said.

Vickie waited impatiently for him to come in that morning, because she had rehearsed all weekend what she would say to him. But he was later than usual. Finally, when several other women strolled out to take a coffee break, she joined them. Sonja, a.k.a. The Source, was among them. Her boyfriend was a policeman; she knew about everything scandalous before anyone else.

As they gathered around the coffee bar, Vickie managed to slip onto the stool beside Sonja, who seemed mildly flattered by the attention. Vickie said, "I haven't seen Teddy today."

Sonja exchanged quick glances with Roberta, on Vickie's other side, and said, "He's getting his new bridgework this morning. Why the interest?"

"No reason," Vickie answered quickly.

Roberta giggled. "Once he has his teeth, we'll have to start watching our rears in the elevator again."

Donna, another of the women, spoke up from the end of the bar. "Sure was nice last week, when he was using the stairs to avoid being seen. Didn't get my tush 'accidentally' brushed against one single time."

Vickie looked around at the others. "Why do we—you put up with it? Why do any of us stand for it?"

Several of the women squirmed and some dropped their gazes, but Sonja answered for everyone. "Teddy's a good software salesman—the best. Winters doesn't like the boat rocked. Besides, Teddy's harmless enough. You just have to have a sense of humor about it."

But Vickie was not so sure. With disgust, seeing she would get no support from her peers, she left them and returned to her cubicle. She got very little work accomplished until Teddy came in shortly before noon, making the rounds with a wide smile to show off his new teeth. He stopped to talk to Sonja, but when he saw Vickie watching, he sauntered over, heels clicking, and leaned into her cubicle. He wasn't, she had to admit grudgingly, a total geek; in fact, with a better personality, he might be considered almost—but no. She gritted her jaw teeth against the thought.

"Hi, doll. I hear you've been asking about me. I didn't know you cared."

Her face grew hot, but she gathered her courage and blurted, "I wanted to know why you were following me Friday night."

His laughter sounded forced. "What makes you think I was? Following you where?"

"You know very well where: in the parking garage." Her voice faltered; perhaps she had made a mistake. Dear God, what a fool she would appear to be. He'd spread it to the whole office. No, it was unthinkable that she could be mistaken.

He shrugged and examined his nails. With envy Vickie noted that they were better buffed than hers, compliments, no doubt, of that randy Japanese manicurist on the first floor.

"Maybe I was just going to my car, same as you."

"Oh? Then why did you slow down and speed up—" For a second it occurred to her that he may have wanted to avoid catching up with her because of his missing bridgework. So maybe he wasn't following her after all. Maybe she was making an utter fool of herself.

But her doubts were dispelled when he reached over and pinched her cheek. "Because you're such a dish, doll, and I like to watch your sweet little haunches gyrate."

He laughed and moved on before she could put her outrage into words.

When she returned from lunch, she found a single, unintelligible syllable on her e-mail screen: *Lurp.* Without thinking to save it, she shuddered and deleted it. He was trying to drive her crazy.

She got up and stalked to his cubicle. He hadn't come back yet. She went out and stood by the elevators, arms crossed, foot tapping. She would stay there if it took all afternoon.

But she didn't have long to wait. When he showed up, twenty minutes late, she cornered him the moment he stepped off the elevator.

"I want to talk to you." She kept her voice at a low growl so that it wouldn't carry inside. Still, a couple of women nearest the door looked up in curiosity.

The new caps flashed. He seemed genuinely pleased. "It's about time to quit playing games, doll."

She kept her tone business-like. "Don't call me 'doll.' I have a name. I expect you to use it."

He nodded affably. "Whatever. You stood out here waiting just to tell me that?"

She hated him for making her feel flustered and unsure of herself. "No—I want—I want to tell you to leave me alone."

His eyes narrowed with interest. "Do you really, now?"

"Yes I do."

"Then tell me something, Miz. Ledbetter. Who's pursuing who? Or, to conform to your nit-picking standards, should I say 'whom'?"

To keep her rage from erupting, she turned on her heel and fled, thinking what an egomaniac he was. She had to concede that he had won this round. True power apparently lies with those who don't seek it. This time she had let him assume the role of victim and thus he had gained the power to manipulate her.

Several times during the afternoon she had to pass his desk. Once he made a pistol with his finger and whispered, "Kapow!" as she walked by.

When she turned quickly away, he spat out what seemed to her a maniacal cackle.

But there were no more messages on her screen that afternoon, and she decided that possibly she had made at least a small impression on him.

As she was locking away her disks, her fax machine coughed out one lone sheet. She almost left it until morning, but at the last minute she picked it up. It wasn't signed, but it originated from the all-night copy store down the block:

Check home mail. Gotcha!

Prickles ran up between her shoulder blades into her hairline. He even knew her home e-mail address. With a growing sense of dread, she cancelled her list of after-work chores and headed straight for her apartment. Leaving her keys dangling in the front door lock, she rushed in and, without even putting down her purse or removing her coat, bent over her computer.

As she feared, a single spammed message, identified only by a string of unintelligible numbers, waited:

On fire with desire. But the wait only multiplies the tension and intensity of the passion.

Her legs trembled so badly she had to sit down. She let out a cry of helpless rage and flipped off the screen, then sank back and tried to breathe. No one, not even Norris—particularly not good, dependable Norris—had ever spoken to her in that manner. For a brief moment she considered phoning Norris, not so much for comfort—for she would never reveal such filth to him: the mere thought brought a flush to her cheeks—but for the sense of stability he brought to her life. Others might look upon his meticulous ways as stodgy, but she functioned best within order, and that is what Norris brought to their relationship. Now, if only Norris were a policeman, like Sonja's guy, instead of an accountant . . . .

But then, no need to call him; just thinking about his steadfastness brought her back to sanity. She could handle this without involving Norris; she simply would not allow that Caplock animal to harass her.

Suddenly chilled for no fathomable reason, she remembered her open door, keys still hanging temptingly in the lock. She jumped up and retrieved them and, taking a quick glance down the hall, shut the door and secured the bolt. Nobody about but that nosey next door neighbor, shuffling toward the trash chute. But old Mrs. Mendel would be of no use if Vickie were ever to cry out for help.

Panic was getting the upper hand. She flicked on the television and tried to push the messages from her mind, assured that she was perfectly safe inside her apartment. And at the office: she was safe there, as well.

A lurid stalker movie drew her to the couch. Almost mindlessly, she curled her feet up, drawing her coat tightly around her, and watched for a full half-hour. Finally, during a long commercial break, hunger intruded itself on her self-imposed masochism, and she broke free of the mood and turned off the set. She went to her kitchenette to eat her yoghurt and cereal, but she had little appetite for food.

Surely there was something Winters could do about it—for one thing, he could call in Gooch, the company computer geek, have him identify the source. Pin Teddy Caplock to the wall. In the meantime, she simply wouldn't read any more messages.

But of course, she had to. At bedtime, almost against her will, she went back to her desk and turned on the computer. A new message glowed in the dark room, sending streaks of terror up to the base of her skull:

I'm going to take you. It won't be rape, you know, because you want it. You know you do.

Then, even as she watched, a second message appeared:

But you won't know when or where. That's what makes this whole situation so so so HOT.

3

A night of disquieting dreams—reliving a lascivious childhood encounter with her cousin Horace in their grandparents' attic under an old quilt, where she first came upon the disgusting discovery of the Male Member—almost caused Vickie to be late to work.

Armed with the latest messages, she marched directly from the elevator, past the crowded coffee bar—noting its high floozie factor—through the maze of staff cubicles, past the golden-eyed secretary Trish, and into Winters' office. He looked up in surprise as she tossed the papers onto his desk.

"What's this?" A tinge of annoyance colored his cheeks, which were pitted and ravaged with acne divots, something that now held new significance.

"I hope you'll choose to act on this." She stood across from him, telegraphing with a glare her determination not to be put off this time. Refraining from playing with her top button.

His fingers edged to the corners of the papers, moving with the speed of a potted nasturtium. He was such a sniveling coward. When his telephone rang, he lit up like a bug-zapper and grabbed it with transparent relief.

"No bother! I'll be right down." He was never so agreeable. He replaced the receiver and grinned in a paunchy charade of regret, blinking rapidly as he always did when he was stonewalling. "Excuse me, Vickie. Something urgent's come up."

He bolted from the office and she followed, protesting, "Like what? You're wanted in surgery?" He passed his astonished secretary, who still held the phone to her ear, and headed through the staff room to the elevators. Vickie was close behind until he left the carpeted offices for the tiled hall.

There she froze, listening to the tap of Winters' heel caps on the hard-surface floor—exactly the sound she'd heard following her. She spun around and went back to his office, explaining to his secretary, who narrowed the dubious golden eyes, "I left something on Russ's desk."

After retrieving the messages, she took a hurried inventory of his work station, mentally scouring the area for some evidence that would tie him to the messages. The locked drawers, where the workers' code names were secreted—might they also contain something more incriminating? Porn magazines, perhaps?

Afraid to arouse Trish's suspicion by tarrying overlong, she returned to her cubicle and stowed the messages in her desk with the others. Could she have been mistaken last Friday night in the parking garage? How could she be sure, now, that it wasn't Winters who followed her, even Winters who wrote the notes? Those pock-marked cheeks suggested a lonely, acne-cursed adolescence that may have left scars on his psyche. Maybe he'd always been starved for the S word. If he were a closet lecher, it would explain why he had been so unresponsive to her complaints—and apparently to the complaints of others, if she could read something more into Sonja's statements of yesterday.

Besides, she knew for certain that Mr. Winters had her home e-mail address, whereas she had no proof that Teddy did. Still, Teddy seemed the more likely suspect; it was hard to imagine Mr. Winters in the role of Lothario. He seldom even looked at her.

A new possibility dawned: maybe Mr. Winters was trying to ease her out, get her to quit. Maybe he had been instructed by upper-management to trim his department. He was such a gutless wonder that this was just the sort of tactic he would take to avoid having to face her and let her go.

I know just the one to begin with, he would say. *And I know precisely how to get rid of her without having to offer her a severance package.*

But she would never resign. Never. Just on principle. She would hang on if she had to bury her teeth in Winters' backside and let him drag her around behind him. If he wanted to fire her, he would have to do it in a manly fashion.

Oh, this was silly. He would never fire her; she was one of his most productive workers. Except that her seniority made her a top wage-earner, as well. She had observed how brutally the company dealt with its loyal employees, turning them out in favor of green novices at lower salaries, or else hiring hourly consultants to save on hospitalization and retirement funds. Oh, she was onto their tactics.

But wait. She was manufacturing scenarios that probably didn't exist, just as she'd probably embellished that childhood tryst under the covers with Horace. It had, after all, begun innocently enough. She and Horace had been rummaging in an old trunk when they had come upon a book of salacious Aubrey Beardsley illustrations of men with grotesquely enormous Hootuses—or was it Hooti? When Horace claimed to have one, too, she didn't believe him. So it had been her fault that he had shown her. Momma had brought that fact home, and Daddy enforced it with several whacks across her behind with the yard stick.

No, it wouldn't be ugly, fat Russ Winters, mainly because she didn't want it to be. Couldn't bear to think about him in that way: an Aubrey Beardsley body with a Russ Winters grapefruit head, sitting at his keyboard late at night composing sexually explicit lust notes to her.

The more logical author was Teddy, of the delicate, fragile ego, who, having had some well-deserved rebuff to his manhood, felt the need to prove himself, and he lacked the confidence to do more than send dirty anonymous messages. She wondered how many of the other women were receiving them. Perhaps she would ask.

Or not. Several of them were such notorious gossips. If they found out, and if she then decided to take retributive action, everyone would know who did it.

Whatever "it" was, Sonja would tell her boyfriend Roscoe, the crackerjack police detective, and he would instantly ferret out the truth.

Unless Vickie were smarter than he, unless he overlooked her completely, unless not even Roscoe would suspect innocent little Vickie of anything worse than blushing at off-color jokes.

She wriggled deeply into her chair with a smug sense of satisfaction. It was too bad she hadn't chosen a life of crime; she was the perfect criminal. Who would think of connecting Victoria Ledbetter with, say, a bank robbery? Or a jewel heist? Or even murder. She was much smarter than people gave her credit for.

Maybe she was even smarter than Roscoe. But it would be too risky to find out, unless she was certain of her anonymity.

Anyway, she would need more time, more evidence, before she ever made a move. When she could positively eliminate her boss as the perpetrator, then, in a civilized manner, she could confront Mr. Winters and demand that he put an end to Teddy's shenanigans, one way or another.

And if he still ignored her, she just might do away with them both. She chuckled secretly at her fantasy.

Then again, maybe Sonja was right; maybe she was making too much of this. After all, what had Teddy done, except be slightly more obnoxious than usual? Well, for one thing, he had hinted at rape.

The thought sent a perverse shudder rattling her very bones.

The office hummed with activity, and she hadn't even booted up yet. She put her dilemma aside and settled into the morning's schedule. But when she checked her e-mail, a chill ran through her bones. There it was again:

I'm watching you. When will it be? God, isn't this suspense orgasmic?

With a gasp, she stood on trembling legs and glanced out her cubicle toward Teddy's. It was empty. And Russ Winters hadn't yet returned. Had he written it last night after she left? Or before she came in this morning? Or just now, from the copy shop in the lobby?

She walked to the adjoining cubicle and asked Fielding, probably the safest, wussiest man in the office, "Seen Teddy?"

Fielding shoved his horn rims up on his nose and flashed an easy conspiratorial grin. "Gone on a call. What? Are you hot for him, too?"

Hot. There was that word again. It stood out in Bold Face, fairly sizzling. She looked around, wondering if anyone else had heard. Without answering, she retreated to her desk in confusion. She was getting paranoid! It couldn't be Fielding: he was in love with Jennifer, the newest woman on the staff. He spent every free minute dogging her, trying to convince her to let him move in, constructing cost-effective graphs about how much money they could save if they were roomies.

But what if he had a secret side—what did she know about him, really? Nothing except that he was no different than any other man. What was he really looking at behind those horn rims?

One thing she had learned in her thirty-four years: they were all craven animals, tools of the Devil. Regardless of their age or educational level, they had to be watched at every turn. A moderately attractive woman like herself was not safe from the mailman, the paperboy, the landlord, her co-workers, even her minister. Momma had warned her many times: "It's your responsibility to guard your virtue. There's a bit of Satan lurking in every man." And Momma hadn't needed to tell her exactly where it lurked.

She wanted to question Mama about whether this applied to Jesus, too, but a certain reticence prevented her. Once she had ventured to ask what Jesus wore under that long robe and received only a shocked frown for her trouble

She went back to her computer and tried to concentrate on her work. But it was useless. She stared into her screen as if it were a crystal ball. But unbidden came the image of naked Horace and the scandal when he was caught with that ridiculous piece of masculine furniture standing expectantly at attention.

Sometime later, Teddy's voice, almost at her elbow, stunned her back to reality. "Again you were asking for me. This is getting serious!" Good grief, he even looked a little like Horace!

She felt her cheeks ignite at the same time her mind blanked; she could think of no excuse for having asked Fielding about him. That rat Fielding must have told him. Or maybe Jennifer or Roberta or Sonja overheard her asking about him. Was there no one she could trust? She turned quickly, brushing a stack of papers with her arm. He grabbed them before they hit the floor. She put her fists in her lap to hide their trembling.

Emboldened by her discomfiture, he laughed and perched on the corner of her desk, aiming his crotch squarely at her, almost at eye level. The inside of her mouth felt as if it were coated with chenille. Her courage evaporated. She was too flustered to be indignant by this new effrontery.

He said, "Maybe you'd like to explain over lunch."

"No!" She said it much too loudly, then, steadying her voice, added, "I'm going to work through lunch today."

"Well, what about after work?"

She shook her head vehemently, swallowing hard past the chenille, avoiding looking at the bulge, the terrible bulge, so near, so near. "It—can wait . . . what I—needed to discuss . . . ."

He was obviously intrigued and in no hurry to leave. Damn him, he knew very well how hard, *hard* it was not to glance at—

In a proprietary gesture, he picked up the framed photo on her desk. "Your parents?"

How dare he sully her parents' picture: Father's condemning glare the same as on that lusty afternoon with Horace; Mother's the same puling acquiescence. She grabbed it and set it down without a word, then returned to her keyboard.

He squirmed back and forth on the desk corner, settling in. She didn't have to look to know what he was doing. "No boyfriend?" he prodded.

She gave him a stiff and disdainful sidelong glance. "I outgrew the 'boyfriend' stage about fifteen years ago. I'm not an adolescent." She refrained from adding *like you.*

"That's obvious." She could feel his gaze lingering on her full breasts. Self-consciously her fingers traveled to her neckline as she felt her nipples prickle. He stood and sauntered out. "If you change your mind, just name the place, doll."

Name the place.

She thought about it for the rest of the day. Yes, that's exactly what she could do. She could name the place, but if he came, smelling heavy of musk, with his bulging twanger, she would be ready. When he made his move, she would—

What?

Her blood surged with the exhilaration of contemplating the possibilities: She could take along a butcher knife and Bobbittize him. Actually, pinking shears would be more creative.

But he would be too strong. No one just lies still for an amputation. How had Lorena Bobbitt managed it?

Besides, all of this presupposed that he would go so far as to expose that dreaded instrument to the light of day, and she'd never allow that to happen. It looked so—whopping, straining there against the gabardine. Her heart pounded just thinking about it, and her breath came in irregular spurts.

Anyway, there could be grave repercussions to deflowering a man. She would go to prison, while some smart surgeon would sew him back together again.

She imagined the delicate stitches.

It would be much wiser to trick him, to trap him into revealing his e-mail authorship, to take her revenge anonymously. But how? The prospect was energizing; it made her breath pump faster. The image of him sitting on her desk—*her* desk—thrusting The Crotch in her face, infuriated her to the point that she could think of nothing else. His audacity was intolerable. She realized how much she despised him, whether he was the letter-writer or not, and how much she longed to delete him. Frag him.

How much she wanted to mutilate him. She squeezed her thighs together, just thinking about it.

If she ever were to act on her fantasies, she would set a trap. For that, she would need his coded e-mail address which Trish kept in a locked drawer. If she confided in Trish—but no. Trish must have given Teddy Vickie's code, or maybe he tricked her into showing him. There was really no one she could be sure of, no one she could trust.

But Victoria Ledbetter could be superior to them all at trickery, outwardly displaying great innocence and naiveté, complete unruffled oblivion to what was going on. But inside, she could be hard as a diamond drill bit.

A little tit for tat. Maybe she could even get wanton, titillating—give her darker side free rein. She could watch his reaction as he read her messages: The corner stool at the coffee bar would offer an unobstructed view of Teddy as he faced his computer. If he was innocent, she would know by his look of puzzlement. If he was guilty, he would know immediately who sent him the message, and it would show all over his face.

In that case, she might lead him on, pretend interest, until she got him to reveal himself irrevocably in an incriminating statement that she could print up and cram down Winters' big fat gullet.

Or she could do as Teddy suggested.

She could name the place.

4

Vickie's options were limited. She could get rid of Teddy, which seemed impossible, or quit her job, move to Canada, change her name. Or she could go ahead and marry Norris Griswold.

One Saturday a month she had dinner with Norris. They had fallen into their understanding by happenstance, when both vacationed alone at a Galveston beachfront hotel three years ago. It was off-season and they kept bumping into each other in the dining room. By the end of the week, they were meeting for a meal in the hotel every evening. They made a pact to continue to the custom each Saturday once they returned to Houston, but after only two evenings they had run out of conversation and mutually agreed that once monthly would be often enough.

Vickie hesitated to break away completely. Norris Griswold would be many women's dream. At thirty-six, he already headed his own plastics firm. His devotion to his widowed mother and to building his business had prevented him from having a serious relationship with a woman until recently. But the business was now flourishing, and the mother had remarried and moved to Carmel, freeing Norris to have a private life.

Vickie's own mother had frowned only imperceptively when she first saw Norris's photograph. Obviously she'd hoped for a more handsome mate for her only daughter. Norris's chin jutted a bit too far and too sharply, and his pale eyes were a little too close together. But he was not as geeky-looking as Vicki had thought when they first met. She had changed her impression as she got to know him, so that she scarcely noticed how he looked. Sometimes, in fact, she could hardly recall his face.

Norris was comfortable to be with, easy to talk to, and a ready escort at a stage in her own career when she had scant time to cultivate friends. Best of all, he demanded very little in the way of intimacy. And anyhow, any old port, as Jesse would say.

Their only semi-sexual encounter—on New Year's Eve that first year—had been the result of too much champagne. They attended an office party at her company but left before midnight. On the way down in the elevator, Vickie, in a fit of alcohol-inspired playfulness, blew into Norris's ear. He responded by grabbing her dress-front and grappling her backward into the wall. But the elevator had mercifully reached the ground floor before he could give her more than a token kiss. She hurriedly straightened her clothes and stepped off the elevator before he could see her rapid breathing. Neither of them ever mentioned the incident again, although she had since dreamed about it more than once. Usually after a heavy, indigestible meal.

Thereafter, they had settled into a routine of Saturday night dinner and a late movie. Usually they met at the restaurant—always the same quiet little Italian cafe on Richmond near the Greenway theater. And, since she had driven there in her own car, they usually parted after the movie and went their separate ways home.

But after the unsettling episode involving Teddy's crotch, to say nothing of his threatening messages on her computer screen, Vickie felt increasingly uneasy about going out alone. So this Saturday she phoned Norris's office and left a message asking him to call for her at her apartment. Usually, if her car was in the shop and she asked him to pick her up, she waited for him at the curb. But this time she asked him to come upstairs for her, even though he would have to find a place to park and perhaps walk a long distance.

His disgruntled expression and the extra jut of his jaw when she opened her door to him confirmed her supposition that he would expect an explanation for this inconvenience. With a twinge of guilt, she even stepped aside and motioned him in, something she almost never did.

"I'm sorry to put you to so much trouble," she said, thinking fast. Originally she had considered telling him she thought it would be raining and didn't want to stand outside in a downpour. But on second thought, she realized that if it had been raining, Norris would have been the one getting wet, and she knew how particular he was about the mirror shine on his shoes.

"I—ah—thought we might have a drink first," she said, watching his irritation melt in surprise.

She shut the door and chained it, then hurried past him into the kitchenette, improvising a cheery excuse as she went. "We've fallen into such a rut lately, I thought it might be fun to—ah—reverse the order. Maybe have a drink and a snack—" She ransacked the tiny cupboard, looking for crackers, nuts, anything that qualified as a snack. "—and catch the early movie, then have dinner later."

She sloshed some Chablis into two somewhat dusty glasses and returned to the living room. He was still standing near the door where she'd left him. With one glass she gestured toward the couch. "Well goodness, have a seat. Where are my manners?"

She set the glasses on the coffee table and returned to the kitchenette to dump some crackers onto a plate. In the refrigerator she found a small cube of Monterrey jack, which she cut the dry end from, then sliced the remaining into thin pieces, arranging them on the plate with the crackers so that they didn't appear skimpy. It didn't look much like a snack that she'd planned ahead of time, but she hoped he wouldn't notice.

When she returned to the living room, Norris was holding a glass aloft, examining it against the light. Quickly she turned the dimmer switch, wishing she'd taken time to dust out the glasses. The shadowy light even made the cheese look better. As if she'd arranged it for atmosphere, she flipped on the radio. Easy Ernie was selling used cars in a frantic falsetto. She flipped over to the classical station; they were playing Beethoven's Funeral March.

With a forced chuckle, she set the plate in front of him. "So much for atmosphere. Well, anyway—" She plopped beside him and reached for a glass. "Cheers!"

Gamely, but with the slightest frown of distaste, Norris brought the glass to his lips, pursing them as though he might somehow be able to sip the contents without actually coming into contact with any contaminants. To prove to him that the glasses were perfectly clean, Vickie turned hers up and drained it while he watched over the rim of his in astonishment. She felt better almost at once.

He took a minute swallow and put his glass down, then reached up and patted the Windsor knot in his tie. It was the blue dotted one this time. Norris alternated between the black and red stripe with his dark grey suit and the navy dot on pale blue with his navy suit.

It occurred to her that he hadn't yet said a single word. Maybe the radio was too overpowering. She jumped up and switched over to easy-listening. Honest Harv was selling pickup trucks. With a shrug of resignation, she turned it off. Norris was gazing toward the far wall, his forehead creased in a puzzled pucker.

She needed another drink, and she figured he did, too. She swept up both glasses and said, "Mercy, look at these old things! Let me get you a sparkly clean one." She whisked them away into the kitchenette and downed the rest of Norris's before washing them both under the hot faucet.

Damn that Teddy Caplock. Maybe she just ought to go out there and confide in Norris the whole thing. But how could she without using suggestive language she could never bring herself to utter, particularly to Norris. And how could she ever describe Teddy's reprehensible conduct in the office, that awful pose of his with his bulging crotch so close—

Hurriedly she dried the glasses and poured the rest of the wine into them, dividing it evenly. Neither was quite full. She ought to fill Norris's to the brim and take the remainder for herself, but she needed it more than he did tonight, after all she'd been through.

As she pushed open the swinging cafe doors with her rump, she felt her bra strap slide down her arm past the edge of her short-sleeved blouse. She sat down carefully and handed Norris his glass and, tipping her own glass to her lips, without thinking ran her free hand into the neck of her blouse to retrieve the strap.

But before she knew what was happening, Norris had gulped down his drink, flung his glass aside with a crash, and dove inside her blouse with both hands, tearing at her bra like a mad man. His hands were followed closely by his nose, nuzzling hotly into her chest. By the time she had collected herself enough to scream, Norris's whole head appeared to be inside her blouse.

"What are you doing?" she yelled, scrambling from under him, giddy from the wine and the burn of Norris's fingers which had penetrated the inner domain perilously close to her bare nipple. The buttons of her blouse lay scattered like petals upon the sofa. She grasped the cloth together with one hand while with the other she pointed toward the door.

"Get out of here!" She was panting so hard that her words came out in a growl.

Norris, who still sat on the couch, examined his hands in wonder as if they might be from another planet. Without looking up, he said hoarsely, "But my word, what was I to think? With all that—activity, I thought you expected me to . . . ."

"Get out!" she screamed even louder, before she remembered that old Mrs. Mendel could hear through their connecting wall.

He rose, walked with precise steps to the door, then turned, thrusting out that damned supercilious chin of his and not quite ever looking any farther than down to the end of his nose. "Does this mean you've changed your mind about the early movie?"

Her breath was still ragged, but she forced it under control, so that her tone would match his measured one. "Yes."

"You just want to go on to dinner first, then?"

An ominous whir from a dark corner of the room sent prickles up the back of her neck bristling into her hairline, although she recognized it at once as the sound of an incoming message on her fax machine. She looked down at the shaking fingers clutching the blouse and expelled a long sigh, willing them to be still.

"Wait in the car until I change."

But the thought of walking any distance alone at night sent new chills through her. Teddy might be waiting, ready to pounce, ready to finish what Norris couldn't. Even Norris ought to offer some protection from him. So she ground her teeth until she could twist her mouth into the semblance of a grim smile.

"On second thought, wait in the hall. Just outside my door."

She shuddered. Her options, it seemed, had narrowed.

5

That she and Norris could revert to their old familiar arm's length stance after such an intimate interlude was precisely the reason—the only reason that Vickie tolerated, sometimes even encouraged the relationship. But Norris would never know the price she paid for overlooking his appalling indiscretion. Outwardly, they ate their meal with the same brisk efficiency as always, even deciding, by dessert, that the previously scheduled movie should be attended, but inside she was still quaking. Occasionally she would allow her gaze to lift from her plate long enough to give him a smoldering glare of despite, which, since he never looked at her, he missed. Animals, she reminded herself. Prurient, loathsome, craven beasts. Every last one. Regardless of whether or not they pointed their crotch.

They passed the short drive to the nearby movie with Norris commenting on the weather and the day's activities, while Vickie knotted her fists in her lap and answered a civil "Um hum" at appropriate intervals.

The film was a foreign one which took her by surprise. The all but illegible English sub-titles were unnecessary; the torrid love scenes told the story. When the female office worker in a very short skirt bent over her desk in a cubicle much like Vickie's, and a co-worker walked up behind her, lifted the skirt and entered her from the rear with the hint of an impossibly enormous Organ, Vickie's esophagus closed off. While the woman on the screen moaned in ecstasy, Vickie grasped her throat and escaped up the aisle to the restroom, where she leaned against the door gasping for breath. Her underclothing was damp, and even in her heightened state of anxiety, she knew that this would never do. She stepped into a stall, removed her undergarment and blotted it repeatedly with tissue until the dampness was gone and she could bear to put it on again. It was a testament to her early training that she was able to return to her seat and watch the rest of the movie as if nothing had happened.

On the drive home, they chose a safe topic, nothing to do with the unspeakable film that Norris had selected. They spoke of the relative merits of Kevin Costner and Tom Cruise, arriving at the conclusion at the precise moment they reached her building that they both preferred Costner.

Ordinarily, she might have allowed him a light peck on the cheek before she got out, but not now. It was understood that he had already had much more than he deserved for the evening—probably for his lifetime—so he didn't even try, to his credit. Nor, to his discredit, did he apologize for his choice of movies.

"Call you next month?" he said almost feebly, but she didn't answer, being consumed with the puzzle of what it was about her that brought out such carnal craving in men.

She let herself into the apartment with some misgiving, dreading to look at that disgusting filth that Teddy had faxed her. She should go on to bed without even reading it, at least until morning, thus sparing herself any more of those horrid, lusty nightmares that his communiqués invariably brought on. In many ways, the man in the film had resembled Teddy. With a shudder, she by-passed her desk and went directly to the kitchenette, where she poured her usual four-ounce portion of buttermilk.

There was no use troubling herself until tomorrow morning. After church. Yes, she would definitely go to church; it had been entirely too long. She hadn't been since the Sunday three weeks ago when, sitting on the first row, she had noticed the rector staring at the space between her knees. She had pressed her legs tightly together and, during the prayer, felt herself swooning in the arms of the Lord. But perhaps the rector had control of his passions by this time. She would try his church again. Her virtue was never in question, but it didn't hurt to remind others of the fact by returning to her pew.

She would go to early service, then stop by for a fresh bagel which she would spread meticulously to the edge with lite cream cheese. She would bring it home, read the papers, then look at Teddy's fax. Thus fortified, so to speak. Although after that horrid movie and Norris's ghastly loss of control, nothing Teddy could say was going to faze her.

She carried her buttermilk through the front room, passing her desk without so much as a downward glance, even though it was burning to be noticed. It was her custom to read in bed for twenty minutes while she drank her buttermilk, and tonight would be no different.

But once she was settled under the covers, she could find absolutely nothing on her bed table that interested her. Maybe there was something on her desk . . . .

She flung back the comforter and padded barefooted into the front room, heart thumping in her throat, probably from buttermilk that was too thick. As she snapped on the desk lamp, her glance naturally fell on the paper in the fax tray. With a relief that bordered on disappointment, she saw on examination that it was a page of figures. She recognized it as the corrections on a project's cost overruns that Jennifer had promised to send her before Monday. The message wasn't signed, but Jennifer, who was new in the office and didn't know better, had sent the message unprotected by the office's elaborate anonymity system, and thus her code name appeared at the top.

Vickie dropped the paper on the desk. Surely Teddy wasn't going to let the entire weekend go by without . . . . Then, realizing she hadn't checked her e-mail, she flipped on her computer and logged in—and there it was: the latest message:

Check out 'Crow' in the Kama Sutra. Can you dig it?

"What kind of pervert does he think I am?" she muttered. Imagine, her owning the *Kama Sutra*. Or even reading it. If only she could fire back an answer and tell him so. But the security system prevented replying to a coded source without manually typing in the recipient's code name.

In disgust, she ran off two copies of the message and put one in her briefcase before going back to bed—without a book. No longer in the mood to read, she lay on her back, staring through the dark at the ceiling.

She would never enter the library and take the *Kama Sutra* from the shelf. Someone might notice. Even if it was a stranger she didn't know, he would have vile thoughts about her. For the same reason, she couldn't order the book from a catalog.

Minutes later she sat up and slapped her forehead. The Internet, of course. She rose and checked the front room blinds to make certain no one could see in before she booted up. As the screen glowed green in the darkened room, she smiled. She wasn't at such a loss as to where to search as everyone would probably have thought—always she imagined a host of her peers standing in a semi-circle observing her life and commenting on it. No, she would tell the gathered observers, I'm not as naive as you think. There was no avoiding overhearing conversations at the office, so that she frequently came into possession of knowledge she had no wish to learn, like how to find the *Kama Sutra* on the Internet, how to pay for a one-time download of a specific section.

It took a full ten minutes before she found the text she was looking for: the definition of "Crow." It was under a section called "Oral Pleasures." As she read the description of the positions of the two partners so as to perform the "Crow", a shiver of disgust ran through her and attached itself to her groin. She pushed away from the desk and breathed deeply, trying to erase the depraved images from her mind. Had people actually done these things?

This confirmed what her pastor had always said about the perversions outside Christianity. There must be a very dark corner of Hell for practitioners of that faith, whatever it was. She would never learn more about exactly what it was, for even that much knowledge might put her in thrall of Satan.

She turned from the screen and opened her briefcase, to see what exactly Teddy had said. As she pulled out his message, her gaze came to rest on the fax from Jennifer with her private code name. The same code name was used for both fax and e-mail. Like Vickie's, Jennifer's code contained a nonsense word. Or was it nonsense? Vickie's was Tishri; Jennifer's was Elul. Elul. Where had she seen that word before, only recently?

The crossword puzzle. She ran to the coffee table, where last Sunday's magazine section still waited, anchored safely under the dictionary. She always saved the puzzle until the following Sunday so that she could check her answers.

With puzzle in hand, she settled in a corner of the sofa under the single lamp that she dared to turn on, and ran her finger across the squares until she found it at twenty-eight Down.

Elul! Now what was the definition? She looked for the clue and read, "Sixth month of the Hebrew calendar."

So if Elul was the name of a Hebrew month, maybe her code word, Tishri, was one as well. She remembered a chart in her dictionary showing Gregorian, Jewish, Muhammadan, and Hindu months, so she flipped through the pages to find the listing for "month." There it was: Tishri, the seventh month in the Hebrew calendar. Only it seemed to correspond to January, the Gregorian first month.

Once in the recent past Mr. Winters had asked her to send him something and had entrusted her with his code name, which she was supposed to destroy immediately thereafter. But one never knew when something disastrous would happen to Mr. Winters and she might be the only one to be able to check his e-mail. So she had saved it. She wondered if it, too, was a Hebrew month. She went to her file and thumbed through until she found it: Adar. It seemed to correspond to the Gregorian month of June.

Anticipation grew. There was an enigma here that she was on the verge of deciphering. She read the month corresponding to July and found Nisan, "the first month of the postexilic calendar; sometimes called the first month of the ecclesiastical year." So the year must end with Adar.

She was very close to discovering something Important. Jennifer Lange's was the sixth month; Vickie Ledbetter's the seventh; Mr. Winters' was the last month.

She recalled that when Jennifer Lange came to work in the office, replacing Bob Laidlaw, Mr. Winters had commented with obvious relief that nobody's code name would have to be changed.

With mounting excitement she grabbed a pencil and began scribbling on a note pad, listing the people in the office, then rearranging them alphabetically: Sonja Abbott, Teddy Caplock, Donna Fromberg, Fielding Goodrich, Leah Haas, Jennifer Lange, Vickie Ledbetter, Trish Morgan, Roberta Shaw, William Somes, Joe Tomlin, and Russ Winters. If each had been assigned a Jewish month as a codeword, then Abbott would be Nisan; Caplock, Iyar; Fromberg, Iwan; Goodrich, Tammuz; Haas, Ab; Lange, Elul; Ledbetter, Tishri; Morgan, Heshvan; Shaw, Kislev; Somes, Teket; Tomlin, Shebat; and Winters, Adar.

Of course her answer would be biblical. It all fit with what she knew. So Teddy would be Iyar, and anything she sent coded Iyar could be opened by him only.

In a surge of glee she returned to the screen, where the *Kama Sutra* beckoned. With the evening's dreadful movie still hovering in her memory, she paged backward until she found "Rear-Entry Positions." She would find an answer to his latest affront that would scorch his drawers—and if he took the bait, she would put an end to his threats and innuendos and outright verbal rape once and for all. It was a justified jihad: a holy war in which the righteous would prevail. She would beat him at his own game and he would be sorry forever.

Or as long as he lived, which wouldn't nearly as long as he'd anticipated.

She typed in his code name and answered his message:

"I dig the *Kama Sutra*. I prefer 'Milch Cow' position. Be at Falcon Park behind the tennis courts—nine o'clock Sunday night."

She took the dictionary back to bed with her and soon fell asleep with the book gripped tightly between her thighs.

6

Morning came too soon, but Vickie fought the urge to stay in bed. She had, after all, determined to go to church, and once a course was set, one must never waver.

It would have been easy to slip into a back pew and not have to suffer the Reverend Clark Wortham's prying eyes, but Vickie did not believe in taking the easy way out of anything. She sat on the first row, as was her wont. Besides, she told her imaginary audience gathered in their perpetual half-circle around her, later, when you're looking for a suspect, you'll remember seeing me in church. I'd be the absolute last one on your list.

Afterward, she spoke to several people on her way out and shook hands with the rector, complimenting him on his sermon. His robe, she noticed at close range, was beginning to get a bit shabby, as was he.

"Good to see you back," he said. Was he flirting? "Will you be joining us for the covered dish supper tonight?" Yes, he was definitely coming on to her. "We'll have a special musical treat."

Pastor Wortham was still smitten, that was obvious. He probably arranged the musical treat especially to entice her into attending. "Oh . . . I don't think so. I have to go in to the office early tomorrow."

"We're always finished by eight," he said. "People stay around to visit, but you'd be free to leave if you needed to."

Vickie brightened. Perfect! An alibi! "In that case, I'll be here." Yes, she would go, but she would keep her distance from the rector. Perhaps eventually he would get over her.

It would be a busy day. On her way to the bagel shop, she stopped at the grocer's for the ingredients for her green bean casserole—always a favorite at the covered dish suppers. During the drive home, a terrible thought occurred: What if Teddy was out of town for the weekend and didn't even get her message? She ought to go by his apartment and check for signs of life.

She knew where he lived because when he moved in the previous year, he threw himself a housewarming party. She hadn't wanted to attend, but Sonja and some of the others had talked her into it: "Aren't you curious to see where it all happens?"

"What 'all happens'?"

"Oh, you know. His many conquests. His deflowering couch."

She had gone, but there was a crush of people, all very boisterous and vulgar. She had fled after some supervisor from Distribution with a whisky breath, gold jewelry, and his shirt unbuttoned halfway down his hairy chest tried to back her into a corner. But now she was glad that she had gone.

His apartment was on the west corner of the second floor. The drapes were drawn, but then he might only be sleeping late. She circled the block and peered into the gated parking area, looking for his red Trans Am. It took several trips, but finally she spotted it, parked at the far end. She sped home, mentally revising her schedule.

After her bagel and a cursory scan of the *Times*, she looked in the Yellow Pages for the nearest camping equipment store. She phoned and got their recorded message that they didn't open until one on Sundays. Although she preferred to fix her green bean casserole just before serving, she went ahead and mixed the ingredients and set them aside in her largest Pyrex dish in the refrigerator, ready to pop into the oven at five.

On second thought, shopping in the nearest camping equipment store was a bad idea. She returned to the phone book and found one on the far north side of town. She didn't bother calling about their hours; it would take the better part of an hour to get there, and it was already noon. Besides, she should stop for money at the ATM and also fill up her gas tank; no sense taking chances on running low before the day was over.

By the time she reached the camping store, it was teeming with customers. Good. No one would even notice her. First she headed for the clothing department and selected a large camouflage poncho, some rain boots and rubber gloves. Then on to the housewares department she went with a bounce to her step. Gone were any niggling reservations about the morality of her action; she was meting out the Lord's vengeance, and it must be so, for wasn't the pastor himself furnishing her with an alibi?

She took some time selecting just the right cast-iron skillet: one with good heft but light enough to wield with ease. She paid for her purchases in cash. Because the skillet was heavy, the clerk put her things in one of the store's large heavy-duty plastic drawstring bags which completely disguised its contents.

Her next stop was a pizza shop, one of those ghastly franchises where, every time a customer walks in, every employee is compelled to call out, "Hi! Welcome to Pepe's!" The young man at the take-out counter had his pencil poised for her order. He looked down her shirt-front, but she quickly buttoned the top button.

She did some mental calculations. "I'll have a fifteen-inch pizza."

"What kind?"

"Umm . . . cheese and mushroom. To go."

The aroma of the shop reminded her of her own hunger. She might just have the pizza for lunch when she got home.

Back in the car with her pizza, she pulled out the skillet and, holding it over the pizza box, saw immediately that she'd made a miscalculation. She hadn't allowed enough room for the handle. But she couldn't go back into the same shop. What would they think?

She drove toward home, looking for another pizza shop. By the time she found one, the late church-goers were streaming in, and she had to wait in line behind several well-dressed couples: men in dark suits and women in carefully correct frocks with medium-high pumps. Micki, who had changed into casual camper attire, felt compelled to explain to the woman behind her, "I went to early service."

"We never go to early service," the woman said. "They use the junior choir. We like the chancel choir and the head organist."

"Good point," Vickie said. To the imaginary semi-circle of investigators, she could say, *I stopped in at Chewy's Pizza and had a conversation with a customer about the merits of the chancel choir. She was . . .* She turned to examine the woman . . . *an older woman with a grey page-boy hair-do, wearing a navy dotted shirtwaist dress and matching navy bag and pumps.*

This time she ordered the jumbo pizza with black olives and cheese. The price was exorbitant. She kept the receipt. *I probably still have the receipt in my purse, if you want proof . . . ah, see? Here it is.*

But then, what would that prove? Well, you never knew what they would ask.

It wasn't too far out of the way to drive by Teddy's again. The drapes were open this time, but the car was gone. Perhaps he went out for lunch, or to get the Sunday paper. Don't forget to check your e-mail, Teddy. But why would he check his coded mail on Sunday? With sinking spirits, she turned toward her apartment.

. . . Unless . . . unless he might be expecting her answer. Of course! He knew she was clever; if he could get her code word, he would figure she could also get his. He was probably waiting for her to reply, and after she did, he would be curious as to the "Milch Cow" reference. Possibly he had gone to the library to look it up. Teddy wasn't the type who would mind someone seeing him take the *Kama Sutra* off the shelf. He also wasn't the type who would own a book—even that one. He probably wasn't even SAVED.

She had already parked the car, but she turned on the engine and drove out again, heading for the branch library nearest to Teddy's place. It was certainly a long shot: he might not even know where the library was. But no, he had to have been there sometime; otherwise, how would he have known about the "Crow"?

She couldn't believe her good fortune: the red Trans Am was parked in the library lot. With a shudder she realized that at that moment he was probably reading about the very prurient activity that had so devastated her at the movie last night: the shocking lifting of the woman's skirt, revealing, not undergarments, but round white buttocks; the deft zip of the man's placket and the falling trousers, disclosing shanks bristling with black hair, like a hog's belly—didn't any of these people wear proper underclothing?—that great protruding tumescent organ, thrusting into the folds of glistening flesh, the hump, hump, hump with wild abandon; the writhing moans of rapture.

With a mighty gasp for air, she whipped the car in a circle in mid-block and sped away, putting as much space as possible between her and the place where Teddy was enacting this odious scene in his imagination.

Still, that she would find his car at the library she took as a sure sign that fate was smiling in broad approval of her plans. They might even fall into the category of a holy war, and surely this was so: She could feel the blessing of the Lord falling like a mantle on her shoulders. For it was well known that the Lord condoned war, but not the other—she could hardly bring herself even to think the S word.

7

The second pizza box was enormous—too large, in fact, but there seemed no alternative; she would have to stuff newspaper around the skillet to keep it from rattling. When she arrived home, she looped the drawstring handle of the camping bag over her arm and put the smaller pizza box atop the larger one, carrying them both in front of her like a serving tray. She would have used the stairs, except the swaying skillet bag kept banging against her leg with every step, threatening to leave her whole side bruised. She hoped to be lucky enough to have the elevator to herself.

But just before the doors had closed completely, old Mrs. Mendel rushed up and pressed the button, causing them to open again. Vickie gave her a grim smile and moved to one side.

"Oy!" Mrs. Mendel's sharp black eyes darted to the boxes. "Someone must be fond of pizza."

"I'm expecting company," Vickie said, marveling that she never noticed before how the elevator fairly lumbered upward.

"Must be a regular party," Mrs. Mendel said. "I hope they won't make a big noisy megillah."

"It's a very sedate group. A—book group. Bible study. You won't even know they're here."

It was possible Mrs. Mendel wouldn't even know what a Bible was. She was probably Jewish.

"My bedroom backs up to your front room," the old woman reminded her. "I like to go to bed early, you know."

"They'll be gone by eight o'clock at the latest," Vickie said. The elevator ground to a bumpy stop at Three and they both stepped off.

As Vickie juggled the boxes reaching for her keys, Mrs. Mendel said, "Do you need some help, dear?"

"No!" She hadn't meant to sound so sharp. "Thanks anyway. I can manage fine . . . ."

She was forced to slip the camping bag from her arm in order to dig into her purse. The bag hit the floor with a clunk. Mrs. Mendel, who was fiddling with her own lock, said, "Looks like someone's going camping, too. Mr. Mendel and I went camping several times with his cousin Joseph. He had a pop-up tent camper that he pulled every winter all the way to Florida. Mr. Mendel loved to go camping, but it wasn't my idea of a way to travel. Like a bunch of gypsies, all that cooking over a fire, and the bugs. And the people! We met the same nushschleppers every year . . . You don't seem like the camping type. It takes a man to be—"

"I'm—just now planning to take it up." Vickie escaped into her apartment and shut the door quickly behind her. Luckily for her, Mrs. Mendel would be long gone to bed before Vickie returned that evening. *I had company that evening*, she told the half-circle of accusers. *We had pizza. You can ask my next-door neighbor.*

By the time she had unloaded her packages, it occurred to her that she couldn't possibly carry all that she would need for both the church and the park down to her car in one trip. Besides, where would she change? Certainly not in the church restroom. She would simply have to lay out her clothing ahead of time, leave the church promptly at eight, rush home, change out of her church dress, pick up her pizza box, stuff the poncho, rubber gloves, and boots in a big garbage bag, and be back in her car by eight-thirty. The drive to the park would take less than fifteen minutes. She would be in position in plenty of time.

Even though they had grown cold, she ate two slices of pizza, one from each box. There was no reason to let the rest go to waste; she put the individual slices into large freezer bags and made room for them between the frozen yogurt and the ice trays. They made a tremendous stack. She would be eating pizza for weeks. Maybe she would invite Norris over.

The afternoon was slipping away. She had barely an hour in which to bathe and dress in her nice blue polyester chiffon with the stole scarf, and lay out a pair of jeans and a gingham shirt to wear later. The matter of shoes posed an unexpected problem. She had planned to change into her rubber-soled walking shoes, but these refused to slide easily in and out of the boots. She settled instead for a pair of brown leather-soled loafers. She wrapped the skillet in some newspaper and put it in the pizza box, picked up the black garbage bag, and placed both box and bag on the bed beside her clothing. She could make the switch in less than five minutes.

At four forty-five, she preheated the oven. At five o'clock she put the foil-covered casserole in to bake. At six o'clock sharp, already wearing her purse over her arm, she put on her oven mitts and removed the casserole.

As she left the apartment, she glanced around once more to be certain she had forgotten nothing. Her gaze lit on the dark computer screen in the corner, but for once it did not beckon. There would be no more intimidating messages from Teddy Caplock.

In the hallway, she placed the dish on the floor and turned the key in the lock, then retrieved the dish and scurried like an attic mouse to the elevator. But despite her attempts at stealth, behind her, the scraping of locks and jingle of chain warned her that Mrs. Mendel was opening her door. She heard, "Your party called off?"

Vickie turned. Mrs. Mendel was peering out a small crack in the doorway. "No. I'm—just—taking this to a sick friend."

Mrs. Mendel stepped into the hall. "Oy, what a mensch, with all you have to do to get ready for your book group." She frowned at the casserole and added, "Must be a very hungry friend."

Vickie looked down at the large oblong dish. "I—I'm taking enough for several days."

"I hope your friend likes leftovers. I never cared for leftovers, myself."

"It tastes even better warmed over," Vickie said lamely.

She finally escaped onto the elevator, heart thumping. But by the time she had driven to the church and found a parking space near the side door, she was in control. She never felt more in control in her life.

During the church supper she all but forgot the rest of the evening's agenda. She made animated small talk with as many of the parishioners as possible; never had she felt so self-assured. But as the hands on the wall clock neared eight o'clock, she began to grow nervous. The singing quartet was holding forth at the front of the parish hall, directly in front of the buffet table. She couldn't interrupt the performers to retrieve her casserole; she would have to leave it.

As she started for the side door, she passed the rector, who was leaning against the wall, arms folded across his chest, enjoying the music. "Leaving so soon?" he whispered.

"Have to. It's eight o'clock." She hoped he detected her accusing tone.

"We'll have someone bring your dish by later."

"No hurry. I'll pick it up next Sunday." She pushed out into the night, a perfect spring evening. The whole plan would have bombed if it had rained.

But there was no time to enjoy it. She hurried to the car and sped off to her apartment. She parked at the curb and, rather than wait on the ancient elevator, took the stairs two at a time in her mid-high heels. This time she was careful to let herself into the apartment quietly, so as not to draw her neighbor to her door again.

Once inside, she glanced at the clock on her desk: eight-twenty. She was five minutes late. She hurried to the bedroom, shucked off her dress and let it fall to the carpet, not even taking time to hang it up. She put on the clothes she had laid out, stepped into the loafers, transferred her keys and wallet to her jeans pocket, grabbed up the garbage bag and the pizza box and rushed to the door, glancing briefly at the clock on her way out: eight twenty-five. Great.

At that moment the phone rang. At first, she thought she wouldn't answer it, but what better alibi could she have? She put down her gear at the door and returned to her desk to check Caller ID. It was Norris. What the—

"Where were you?" Her mother used to use the same accusing tone. "I've tried three times before . . ."

"I went to the church supper. Look—" She was breathless.

"All day? I called early this afternoon."

"I went to the store. Guess I forgot to check Caller ID when I came in. Norris, I can't talk now."

"Can't you spare me a minute?" He sounded like the pathetic wimp that he was. "I only want to apologize for last night."

"There's no need," she said shortly. "It's forgotten." For emphasis, she added, "Really. Now I have to—"

His voice rose, quavering. "You mean it? Oh God, Vickie, I am . . . well . . . vastly relieved!"

"Yeah, well . . ." She stood on one foot and then the other. She should have left time to pee in her schedule.

"I mean the whole evening was such a disaster. And that movie!"

"Please, Norris. Don't mention that movie."

"With all that nudity—"

"I have to go, Norris!"

"—and orgiastic sex—"

"I can't talk now! I'll phone you later." She slammed down the receiver, then took it off the hook again, in case he should call back. Eight thirty-one. With trembling hands, she picked up the bag and box and let herself silently out of the apartment.

As she tiptoed toward the stairwell, the elevator doors opened and out stepped Mrs. Mendel. "Another sick friend?" she called.

Vickie froze, then forced herself to turn and smile. "Actually, one of the members of the book club . . . fell down . . . and broke a bone. So we're moving our meeting to her place." She held up the pizza box as if to prove it.

"Funny," the old woman said. "I thought you said the meeting would be over by this time."

"We are . . . getting a late start . . . because of the accident." Vickie could feel her bladder filling by the minute.

Mrs. Mendel eyed the plastic bag. "You got your books in there, I suppose."

Vickie swallowed. "Yes. Yes I do."

"That's a big bag. You must have lots of books."

Vickie decided to use the elevator, just to escape. She stepped on and pushed the button. "Good night, Mrs. Mendel."

"It must be a very informal gathering, judging by your clothes," Mrs. Mendel called as the doors slowly slid together.

Vickie glanced at her watch. Less than thirty minutes. Teddy would probably be early, to boot. She had to be dressed in poncho and boots and be in place, out of sight, by eight forty-five.

"I'll never make it," she breathed. But she had to.

She drove as swiftly as possible without breaking too many laws, darting in and out of lanes, squeezing through on yellow lights, screeching around corners, coming at last to Falcon Park at eight forty-six. Not bad. She parked at the end of the lot, away from the halogen light illuminating the area; grabbed up her gear, and raced to the tennis courts.

But as she reached the rear of the courts where the lone bench sat among the bushes, she was brought up short in horror:

Someone was using the bench. A man with jeans bunched around his ankles held a woman on his lap. Her skirt was waist-high, her legs were wrapped around him, and his hands cupped her bare buttocks. Her unbuttoned blouse slid off one shoulder so that Vickie could see the man's mouth closed around one plump breast. The woman, who kept slithering sideways back and forth, threw her head back and sobbed out, "Oh my God, oh my God . . . don't stop!"

Vickie sucked her breath in a sharp moan. She could come to no other rational conclusion but that they were Doing It right there in public!

8

While the couple pumped and rutted like common farm animals, Vickie, in great glandular distress, worked her cautious way around to the bushes behind them, fretting about how she could bring about a conclusion to their activity. By now she had determined that the man bore no resemblance to Teddy. But there wasn't much time before Teddy would appear. Perhaps if she cleared her throat discretely, they would be overcome with embarrassment and leave.

She backed deep into the bushes and said, "Ahem."

But the woman groaned in randy ecstasy and the rhythmic rocking continued. The man increased his nibbling, which was interspersed with gasps of, "Doris. Oh babe! Doris!" Vickie's panic, along with her nausea, escalated. Never, not even in the movies, had she witnessed such carnal abandon. It was the most ghastly experience of her life. She felt something brush her head, and when she looked up to see, discovered a pair of red lace bikinis which had been flung onto the tree limb. She jumped back as if she had been stung. Her head buzzed, and she thought she might faint.

When she could stand it no longer, with the last ounce of strength remaining, she shrieked, "Stop it!" But they didn't hear.

At that same instant the woman howled, "Oh God in heaven!" then shuddered, groaned, panted, and collapsed against the man's chest.

He gasped, "Thank God you're through! You like to of wore me out!"

He rolled her off his lap and stood, pulling on his trousers and mooning Vickie in the process. But the woman had no such inclination toward modesty. She lay splayed on the bench, blouse akimbo, skirt bunched around her waist. One arm lolled off the bench and two fingers waggled back and forth.

"I need a smoke," she said.

He felt of his chest pocket and said, "Must've left them on the bike." He plunged off toward the parking lot, leaving the woman humming some lyrics from a Wynona tune.

Vickie sighed in relief. Maybe they would be gone by the time Teddy showed up, after all. With as much stealth as she could manage, she laid down the pizza box and the plastic bag. It made a crinkling sound as it settled onto the ground, but the woman reached a soulful crescendo in the Wynona song, so Vickie cautiously opened it, bit by bit, until she could pull out the poncho.

Suddenly the singing stopped. The woman said, "Is that you, Carl?" Vickie froze.

But it wasn't Vickie the woman heard. Into the clearing Teddy stepped, and for only a moment his face was caught in the tennis court lights before he moved beyond them. In that brief second, Vickie saw a look of incredulity, as if he couldn't believe his good fortune. As he rushed forward, he unfastened his trousers with more speed than Vickie imagined possible, allowing them to fall to his ankles, so that he had to hobble the last few steps, arms thrown wide in welcome. Vickie shivered in revulsion. His belly was covered with black hair, which grew thicker as it reached The Organ.

"Man, oh man, I was ready for the Milch Cow, but I damn sure didn't expect this!" He said it just before he threw himself upon the woman. She had jerked up at the last minute, belatedly realizing that Teddy was not her lover, and began screaming and flailing both arms and legs in an attempt to ward off her attacker. In mid thrust, he looked puzzled and stopped long enough to say, "Who are you?"

Vickie could have sung the Hallelujah Chorus for all anyone would have noticed, but she knew she must be ready to act, if this opportunity were not to be wasted. She shook so hard that she had trouble slipping on her poncho, rubber gloves and boots. She kicked the empty bag aside. Her heart hammered violently and she actually forgot herself and cried out in disgust at the spectacle before her, but no one heard.

At that moment, Carl, bellowing a primal territorial yell, burst through the bushes, grabbed Teddy by the back of his shirt, spun him around, and hit him so hard Vickie could hear his jaw crack.

"Get offa my woman, you lowdown sonofa—!"

Teddy crumbled onto the bench, moaning, "What the hell is this all about?"

Carl jerked the woman to her feet. "Come on, Doris. Let's get out of here. Goddam perverts! They're everywhere!"

On the run, the woman tried to pick up her shoes from the ground and said, "But my shoes! My thong panties!"

"Hell, I'll buy you new ones."

Vickie, in a seething purple rage, knew in her soul that Teddy had meant to attack her. All along she had known it. If she hadn't been clever at deciphering his e-mail identity, she would be the one he would have pointed that awful instrument at. With trembling fingers, she opened the pizza box and drew out the iron skillet. As the motorcycle roared away, she crept up behind the bench and, with both hands, lifted the skillet over her head.

He must have heard her, for he turned and looked directly into her eyes. She had no choice then. If she had doubted her ability to go through with it, once he had seen her face, she had to act. With all her strength she closed her eyes and brought the skillet down against his skull, hearing bone crack. Whack. It sounded like iron splintering wood. And again, boing, boing, boing, until she could barely lift it, could scarcely control the jerkiness of her arms. What was once the top of Teddy's head now glistened in the moonlight: a bloody mushy nub.

As she had anticipated, blood spurted everywhere, covering her poncho and boots. With ratchety gulps of air, shaking so that any planned movement was an effort, she backed away until the safety of the bushes enveloped her. Again the red lace thong panties slapped her face, but she gave them a vicious bat with her skillet and knocked them to the ground. Then, forcing herself to get a grip, with the utmost care, she rewrapped the skillet in the newspaper and put it back into the pizza box. Then she took off the poncho, boots, and gloves, and placed them in the plastic bag.

By the time she had worked her circuitous way back to the parking lot, her breathing and heartbeat had almost returned to normal, although her knees still threatened to buckle with each step. But she was okay—better than she would have been if Teddy had gotten hold of her.

Her foot shook against the accelerator. Careful not to exceed the speed limit, she drove for several miles until she found an apartment dumpster, into which she deposited the plastic garbage bag. Now how to dispose of the pizza box.

She wasn't too far from the Central River Bridge that bisected the city. That seemed the most likely spot. Strange that she hadn't thought this out ahead of time. She realized now that all during her meticulous planning, she hadn't been sure that she would actually do it, hadn't known whether she would really be forced to use the skillet. She'd only brought it for self-defense, she told herself. If the couple hadn't driven her crazy, or if Teddy had been different . . . but that awful display, the menacing nether member just standing at attention in full view. She shuddered again. No, she had no choice. No choice whatsoever.

Once she reached the bridge, she turned on her hazard lights and waited until there were no other cars in sight. Then she got out only long enough to drop the box over the railing. With satisfaction she listened as it broke the water surface with a loud, distant plop.

She returned to her car almost smiling, trying to remember the lyrics to the Wynona song. She could be proud of herself this night for keeping her head. Justice had prevailed, and she had been its instrument.

"Praise the Lord," she breathed.

9

Well past midnight, when it became apparent that her adrenalin would never stop pumping without help, Vickie got up and downed a half-glass of brandy, kept on hand for medicinal purposes. Thus she incorporated the sound of her alarm clock into her nightmare, in which it became the grade school fire alarm. In her dream, she was being punished for some minor infraction by being forced to stand in the corner and wasn't allowed to flee the burning building with the other students. She was often troubled by dreams in which she was punished for disobeying an impossibly difficult slate of rules, while close by her Aunt Jesse would be performing some wanton act of depravity in full view of the principal without receiving even the slightest rebuke.

When she awoke, almost an hour past time to get up, she realized that there was no way she could avoid being late for work. It would be her first violation of the office's schedule, ever.

While she scurried from bedroom to bath to kitchenette, waiting for the iron to heat so that she could put a fresh crease in her jacket sleeves—something she should have done after she last wore it—she flipped on the radio, even though she was fairly certain that it would be too soon for Teddy's body to be found.

But she was mistaken. The newscaster's report came on in mid-sentence: "—are investigating the physical evidence found at the scene of the brutal beating, which consisted of a pair of women's shoes, we are told, and an item of intimate apparel. Police speculate, from the victim's state of undress, and from the fact that his wallet and jewelry were untouched, that it was a crime of passion. And now a look at sports . . . ."

So soon . . . so soon. She wondered who had come upon his body, and when. Maybe the woman had persuaded the man on the motorcycle to go back to look for her shoes. Maybe they had seen the body and fled, but later decided to call the police. Or maybe a policeman on his beat had wandered by . . . . She took a moment to scan the morning paper, but could find no mention of the crime.

On the way to work, she flicked on the car radio, hoping to hear more. But all she could find were music and traffic reports.

She was flushed and panting by the time she reached the office. Several of the employees were gathered around the coffee bar, but they paid her late arrival scant attention. Except for the secretary Trish, who eyed her with interest.

"Well would you look who's dragging in late for the very first time! What happened to you? Have a late date?" Several of the women giggled when she said it.

Without giving it enough thought, she blurted, "I—was listening to the shocking news about Teddy."

"What news?" Sonja asked. "Nothing Teddy does shocks me anymore."

Vickie looked from one to the other of the women, blinking. *My Lord, they don't know. Doesn't anyone listen to the news?* Or had the victim's name not been released, pending notification of the next of kin? She swallowed back her panic. *Good grief, that's it! They didn't mention Teddy by name. What have I done?* She tried to think how to answer, but her tongue was frozen with fright. Her hands shook so hard that she had to grasp them together to control the tremors.

Trish said, "Hey, are you all right? You look pretty strung out."

"I had a bad night . . . . Something I ate at the church supper. Maybe I'd better sit down." She fled to her cubicle, sick with fright. *Be careful, Vickie. Wait until they mention it to you.*

The others quickly forgot about her, she could tell by the tone of their talk. Or had they? It was punctuated by frequent laughter. Maybe they were talking about her. Making fun of her. Often she'd had the feeling that the others derided her piety. The preacher frequently warned his congregation about hard it was to avoid the snares of Satan.

When her phone rang, she was almost relieved. But she was unprepared to hear Norris's anxious voice; she was too stunned, in fact, to be annoyed. Norris never called her at work except on every other Friday afternoon to confirm their dinner date for Saturday.

She could not keep from sounding cross. "What in the world do you want at this hour?"

"I was worried. I called again last night but your line was busy for hours."

"I was talking to an old friend."

"In the dark? I got so worried that I drove over and saw that all your lights were out."

"After we hung up, I—wasn't feeling well. I left the phone off the hook and went straight to bed and fell to sleep immediately." She struggled to regain the upper hand. "Are you stalking me, Norris?"

Perhaps he didn't hear her. "—but your car wasn't there."

She wiped the perspiration from her upper lip. "Oh . . . I forgot. I—was out of milk. I needed a glass of warm milk to help me sleep. I went out for just a minute to the grocery store."

"You sound angry. Are you, still?"

"No, no of course not," she snapped. "I'm just tired—very tired."

He was silent for a moment. "After all that sleep? You're not coming down with something, are you? You sound peculiar."

Her guilt must show in her voice. Why must he ask so many questions? Norris was becoming entirely too possessive. She said, "If you must know, something terrible happened to someone in our office, and it's—just—upsetting."

"Terrible?" He was obviously fishing for more. The creep.

"I don't want to talk about it. I have to hang up now."

"Wait! Can I—may I come by this evening just for a few minutes?"

"Whatever for? I don't think so." Impatiently she turned on her computer and unlocked her desk to take out her program disk.

"It won't take long. I just want to bring you—"

"Norris, I am trying to work here!" Angrily she flicked onto her e-mail. Then she sucked in her breath in horror at the message on her screen:

The Crow is waiting for you, babycakes.

A quavering moan of terror escaped her lips.

"Vickie? Are you still there? What was that noise? Are you all right?"

Her whole body had gone rigid. Teddy was dead; she knew he was dead. But for a chilling moment she pictured his zombie corpse rising from that bench, blood streaming from his battered head, staggering to his car, trousers still around his ankles, the magnificent grotesque organ pointing the way—it had achieved monumental proportions in her mind—driving to his apartment.

No, the newscaster had said his body was found in the park. Hadn't he said that? Yes, there was something about the woman's bikini panties, so it must have been in the park.

Or maybe he had his laptop in the car, and managed to reach it to send her one last e-mail message.

Or was it the last? Would he continue to haunt her throughout eternity? *Is this what Hell is all about?*

With a fit of convulsive shakes, she fought off the image of succumbing to the "Crow" at the hands of a bloody cadaver.

She stammered into the phone, "On second thought, yes. Come over after work. Come as soon as possible."

10

Vicki sat at her desk for hours, gazing at a small photo of her unflappable Aunt Jesse, wondering how she would handle the situation, drawing from Jesse's strength. By noontime, common sense had reasserted itself and she was able to turn her thoughts to work. She realized she had neglected completely checking her e-mail on Sunday. Obviously Teddy wrote the message sometime before he went out to meet her at Falcon Park, maybe even as early as Saturday night. With that thought and the routine of the business day to catch up on, her panic gradually subsided.

Until Sonja's boyfriend showed up.

His name was Roscoe, and he was with the police department. She had seen him at several office parties. Roscoe and Sonja had been dating for about three years, as Vickie calculated. He and Teddy were teammates in a local bowling league, but Vickie was not certain which relationship had come first: whether Teddy introduced him to Sonja, or Sonja introduced him to Teddy. Somehow, the two men seemed inordinately thick.

But Roscoe didn't come to see Sonja. Instead, he went directly to Russ Winters' office where Trish ushered him in as if he were expected. From her cubicle Vickie couldn't watch what was going on without peering over the top, so she grabbed some papers and hurried to the copy machine near Trish's desk. This machine was for the secretary's private use, but sometimes in a pinch, when all the machines in the copy room were in use, some of the staff would borrow Trish's—although Vickie never had before.

Roscoe didn't stay long, and when he came out, he stopped only briefly at Sonja's cubicle, then left. It didn't look like a communication between lovers. Vickie could tell, from the somber look on his face, that he had delivered bad news.

Bad news for everyone but her.

Mr. Winters, who had escorted Roscoe to his door, turned to Trish and said, "Tell Joe Tomlin I want to see him."

Vickie knew exactly what was on Russ Winters' mind. Joe Tomlin was, at fifty, the oldest man—the oldest person—in the office. The others, Vickie included, looked upon him as a dweeb for not having advanced into the upper echelons of the company after many years of service. He seemed content to languish in obscurity. Obviously he was not ambitious: he had let his hair go grey and recede, never bothering to dye it or even use Rogaine. The coffee bar loungers often discussed this in amazement. His ties were the same ones he had worn year in and year out, and his wife wore the same red sequined dress to every office Christmas party. Joe Tomlin had been here even longer than Mr. Winters. So it stood to reason that he would be chosen to assume Teddy's workload.

To stretch time, Vickie took pains to refill every paper tray before she began copying. She dawdled so long that Trish began eyeing her with curiosity, so with great reluctance she returned to her cubicle.

What were they saying in there? Maybe Russ was giving Joe a description of Teddy's bloody condition, one that she hadn't been able to see clearly by the single overhead light in the park. But then, it was just as well. The sight of blood always nauseated her.

She listened intently for the sound of Winters' door opening, and then she rushed back to the copy machine. At Trish's questioning gaze, she explained, "I must've left my pen here." She made great pretense of searching the floor around the machine as Joe came out. He had a properly stunned look as he turned and said to Mr. Winters, "I'll do my best. That's all I can promise. But I hope you'll ask the others to share the load."

"Okay. I'll work on it now." Winters frowned toward Vickie as he beckoned to Trish. "See you in my office?" It wasn't a question.

Vickie fell in beside Joe as he headed—not back to his cubicle, but toward the elevators. She knew exactly where he was going: down to the lobby to smoke. She got on the elevator with him and said, "I couldn't help but hear. Sounds like Russ is piling extra chores on you. It must be tough being the one with the most experience."

He ran his hand over his forehead and up his balding head. "Yeah. I have to absorb some of Teddy's accounts. Did you hear the newscast about that beating victim in the park? It was Teddy."

She was glad to be able to try out her astonishment on good old indiscriminant Joe first. "Oh my gosh, how awful! Such a tragedy! Do they know who did it?"

"They may have gotten lucky on that one. Russ says there were some clues at the scene: a pair of women's shoes, for one thing. Roscoe told him a couple on a motorcycle was stopped last night for speeding. The officer who ticketed them noticed the woman didn't have on any shoes. Soon after Teddy was found, they put out an APB to pick them up. Only a matter of time, I figure."

Vickie's head was ringing with peals of hosannas. She couldn't believe her good fortune. Obviously the fates were smiling on her, vindicating her. She went to the lobby newsstand and picked up a candy bar, then hurried back upstairs, a brilliant plan already forming. What were the names she'd heard the two fornicators use? She would never forget the man's "Doris, Doris, Doris" as he pumped away inside her. But his name? The harlot had used it only once—Earl? No . . . Carl!

She went to her cubicle and watched until Sonja left for the restroom, then she got up and followed. Fortunately, the restroom was empty except for the two of them.

She entered the stall next to Sonja's and said, "Joe told me about poor Teddy—guess Roscoe told you."

"Yes. I didn't know whether to mention it or not. Sometimes what Roscoe tells me is confidential."

"I guess that jealous ex-boyfriend of Doris's got to Teddy, after all. What's his name? Oh yeah: Carl. I warned Teddy he ought to be careful, but—" She flushed the toilet and strolled out to the lavatories, waiting for Sonja to take the bait.

Sonja appeared at her side, deep-set eyes wide, looking at her in the mirror. "What are you talking about? Who's Doris?"

"You know . . . or maybe you don't. Teddy tried to keep their relationship low-key, because her ex was such a wild man. I happened to witness one of his blowups when he found the two of them together."

The dark eyes glinted with disbelief. "I didn't know you and Teddy were such great friends."

"We weren't. I just happened to meet them once outside the . . . movies. Teddy introduced me to Doris—he'd mentioned her to me once or twice before—and about that time this brute named Carl rode up on a motorcycle. Right there, in plain view of everyone, he threatened to beat Teddy to a pulp if he didn't leave Doris alone." *There is no sin in a lie that causes Right to prevail.*

"So you know what he looks like?"

"Oh definitely. I'd know him anywhere. Her, too." There. Enough said. Don't want to string it out too long. She hurried out ahead of Sonja and retreated to her desk.

Mr. Winters had just stepped out of his office. He cleared his throat and raised his voice. "Could I have everyone's attention up here, please?"

There was silence. One by one the men and women came out of their cubicles and shuffled to the front of the room, like reluctant robots. Vickie moved boldly to one side of the semi-circle that formed around Winters.

His gaze swept the group and came to rest, she felt, upon her. "Some of you may have heard the bad news," he said. "The victim of that vicious beating at Falcon Park last night was Teddy Caplock."

Several gasped in disbelief. Vickie, turning so that she could watch their faces, mimicked their reaction.

"For now, Joe will take over the Galloway account. I expect the rest of you will have to assume other of Teddy's duties for a short while."

His words were drowned out in the confusion of voices that rose with questions.

"Do they know who did it?" Fielding asked.

Sonja, who had joined the group at the opposite side, said, "Roscoe says they have a suspect."

"That was quick," Fielding said. "Who is it?"

She shrugged. "He didn't say. I don't think they have anyone in custody yet. But Vickie—" She frowned, narrowed eyes lit with recollection and fixed on Vickie. "Say! Weren't you talking about this when you first came in this morning?"

Chatter stopped abruptly, and those who had been gathered at the coffee bar that morning fixed inquisitive gazes boring into her. She was afraid they would hear the thumping of her heart.

"No!" she blustered. "How could I?"

Donna Fromberg butted in. "You said something terrible had happened to Teddy. I distinctly remember—"

Vickie forced a laugh. "Oh that! That had nothing to do with this." She looked around the group, avoiding eyes, concentrating on feet, groping for a way to change the subject. She clasped her hands behind her back to hide their violent shaking.

"Then what were you talking about?" Sonja insisted.

"It was . . . something entirely different, something really silly and petty compared to this." Suddenly seized by inspiration, she added somberly, "But it doesn't seem right—or respectful—to talk about it, now that he's dead."

Russ Winters broke in. "Oh, I must've given you the wrong impression. Teddy's not dead. They've been operating all night, repairing his skull. Roscoe says Teddy's made of stern stuff. He has a good chance of pulling through."

11

Vickie left work an hour early, claiming illness. It was no exaggeration: her forehead, hot to the touch, throbbed with an unremitting pain. Her throat was so constricted that it hurt, and her tongue felt swollen. If Teddy survived, she would have to flee. Even if he ultimately died, if he regained consciousness long enough to accuse her, she would still have to run, would have to change her name and go—where? And how would she live?

Twice before she left the office, she phoned the hospital but could get no information beyond that his condition was critical. He was in intensive care, and visitors outside the immediate family would not be admitted. She did not know he had any family; even now she could not picture him as having once been a child, with parents who loved him, with siblings with whom he alternately bickered and played. These images warred with what she knew to be true about him: he was a depraved sex monger.

As she entered the apartment elevator, it occurred to her that Teddy's family, if they were from out of town, might gather at his place. Possibly she could call there and glean some information that would help her make a decision as to what action to take.

She had come to suspect everyone; she eyed the three other people on the elevator warily, halfway expecting the police to be after her already. But she soon realized that they were all tenants she recognized.

Then, just before the doors closed, Norris came rushing up, breathless. He smiled and edged in beside her. "I called your office. They said you'd left early, not feeling well. So I came right over."

Damn. She had forgotten that earlier in the day, when the e-mail message that seemed to come from the grave had left her in a panic, she had invited him to come. Now she couldn't rebuff him, couldn't tell him in front of the other passengers, that she didn't want him here. They were all smiling benignly at their feet or at the ceiling or the elevator doors, pretending not to hear, but thinking, no doubt, what a thoughtful young man she had. He leaned close to her ear, blowing his Juicy Fruit breath into her face. "You don't seem glad to see me. Not still mad, are you?"

She swallowed to keep from gagging. There was a time when she had liked the smell of Juicy Fruit. "I'm coming down with something. Maybe you shouldn't go upstairs." She said it loudly enough for everyone to hear and noted with satisfaction how they moved a step away, crowing against one another in an effort to escape her germs, leaving her and Norris on an island of space in the center of the elevator.

He touched her cheek in a gesture that she feared the other passengers would misconstrue as intimate. "You're warm. I'll fix you some soup, at least."

She was too traumatized to argue. As the doors opened at Three, he took her elbow and guided her out—into the path of Mrs. Mendel, who was headed toward the trash chute with a plastic bag.

The old woman nodded at him with just a hint of disapproval, then turned to Vickie. "How did your book club enjoy the pizza last night, dolling?"

"What? Oh—Fine." Vickie dug frantically into her bag in search of her door key, trying to remember what she'd told Mrs. Mendel.

Mrs. Mendel again attacked Norris with a fishy glare, until he squirmed and put in, "She doesn't feel well. I think she has a fever."

"Oy too bad," Mrs. Mendel said. "Well it's no wonder. When you went out last night with nothing but that little gingham shirt, I said to myself, 'That girl's going to catch her death.'"

The woman had a forty gigabyte memory. Vickie got the door open and hurried inside, leaving Norris to deal with Mrs. Mendel. She heard the old woman say, "Why don't I fix her one of my special hot toddies? I used to give them to Mr. Mendel when he got any kind of symptoms whatsoever—kidney stones, upset stomach, diarrhea."

"That would be nice, thanks," he said.

Oh great. Why would he say that? Now she would have both of them underfoot. When he came inside and closed the door, she said, "I'm going to bed. I'm counting on you not to let that woman into this apartment."

He followed her to the bedroom door. "Vickie? Didn't you tell me you went to a church supper last night?"

"I—I did. That old woman is senile. She gets things all mixed up."

He nodded thoughtfully. "Right . . . . Because you don't even belong to a book club, do you?"

The doorbell startled them both. He said, "That's the fastest toddy I ever saw." But when he opened the door, even though Vickie couldn't see, she could tell immediately that it wasn't Mrs. Mendel. The voice was that of a man, and he sounded surprised.

"Hello there. I hope I have the right apartment. I'm looking for Vickie."

Good lord. The rector. So he was after her too. Was every man she knew in heat?

Norris sounded the least bit testy. "This is her place. She's not feeling well enough for visitors."

"I'm sorry. I'm Clark Wortham, rector at St. Timothy's. I'm returning Vickie's dish. As usual, everyone loved her bean casserole."

Vickie sighed. In any case, the rector was corroborating her story of her whereabouts the night before.

"Oh—and I think she lost this scarf, or stole, or whatever. It must be hers; it matches the dress she had on last night."

Norris's voice was strained. The poor wimp couldn't take the least competition. "Yes. I recognize it. Thanks. I'll tell Vickie you stopped by."

Vickie glanced at her dress, still crumpled on the floor. She hadn't even missed the stole. What had gotten into her, leaving her clothes lying around? In all her life she had never done anything even remotely that careless before. Hurriedly, she picked up the dress and took it to the closet.

Norris returned to the bedroom door carrying the stole and the dish. "This is your scarf, isn't it?"

She closed the closet. "Yes, I hadn't even missed it."

He came into her room and handed her the stole. "Must've been some night. Anyway, I thought Mrs. Mendel said you had on a gingham shirt."

She coughed to cover her momentary dilemma. "That just shows how confused she is." She thought quickly. "Come to think of it, I believe I went to a book store the night before that; Mrs. Mendel probably heard me wrong and thought I said club. The poor woman is dotty. She lost a whole day." There. That ought to satisfy the twit.

But still he stood there, frowning. If she had a butcher knife, she would run him through right then. How was she going to get him out of her room? Men were so lusty; just being near a bed gave them ideas, all of them. That's what Aunt Jesse told her years ago.

He didn't move. "She said you took pizza, too."

Her laugh sounded phony, even to her. "Imagine me taking pizza to a church supper! Anyway, I hate the whole idea of pizza, and you know it."

Still he didn't leave. She said, "Put the dish in the kitchen. There'll be no need to make soup if Mrs. Mendel—"

At that moment the doorbell rang again and Norris went to answer it. Vickie sat on the side of the bed, waiting for some privacy so that she could phone Teddy's apartment.

It was Mrs. Mendel, and she could tell by the sound that it was the advancing Mrs. Mendel, Norris obviously being powerless to head her off. She was addressing him almost accusingly—or was it sarcastically? "Oh, so you were the sick friend Vickie fixed that casserole for."

"Huh?" he said dumbly.

"But I thought it was a girl friend, with a broken leg or something."

"I don't know what you're talking about," he said.

Vickie could hear Mrs. Mendel bearing down, and almost immediately she invaded the bedroom, wrinkled face beaming above the steaming mug.

"Here we are! That's right, take off those shoes and slide under the covers and drink this. Sip it slowly and inhale the vapors. They're good for the lungs."

Vickie's lungs were being clamped by a tight band that no toddy was going to loosen. But she did as she was told and took the mug, gulping a big mouthful, wishing it would render her unconscious. The warm liquid seared as it went down, but almost immediately she began to feel better in spite of everything. Probably just tension, she realized. It was not a propitious moment to get sick, when she needed all her faculties.

To his credit, Norris appeared behind the old woman and said in as commanding tone as he possessed, "Maybe we should let her get some rest."

Mrs. Mendel nodded, but made no move to leave. "Incidentally, I just heard on the news: you know that terrible beating in the park last night?"

Vickie perked up, and a shiver of anticipation ran up her spine. "Yes." Maybe he's dead, dear God. If there is justice in the world . . . .

"They announced the poor victim's identity. It's someone that works at your company, did you know that?"

"No . . . no. I didn't know that." Vickie returned to her toddy, bending her head low over the mug, hands shaking.

Norris took Mrs. Mendel by the arm, but as she was being led away, she called back, "Caplock, I believe it was. Do you know anyone by the name of—?"

Norris, evincing a firmness she didn't know he had, said, "Thank you for the toddy, Mrs. Mendel. I'll return the mug."

They were out of sight, but Vickie could imagine Mrs. Mendel's cold appraisal. "You're not planning to stay here, I hope—with that girl tanked up on whisky—"

"Of course not. No longer than I'm needed. But I'll wash and return your mug before I leave."

"You might fix an ice bag for her fever. Mr. Mendel used to like—"

"Thank you. Good idea," he said, closing the door while she was still speaking.

As Vickie leaned against the pillows and sipped the toddy, a great idea was taking form. She called out, "Norris?" He appeared instantly. "Would you make a call for me? We do have a Caplock in our office; you may have met him at the parties—tall, dark-headed, good—" She swallowed and clenched her buttocks together beneath the covers. "Some people might say nice-looking. Would you call his apartment to check on how he is? The number's in my address book on the desk."

"I think I remember him," he said. The perpetual frown deepened as he turned to leave. "Cheeky sort, if I recall."

Great. Much better if a man checks on Teddy, in case the police are listening in. They're probably looking for a man, anyway.

The mug was half empty by the time he returned, shaking his head. "No luck," he said.

"Would you try the hospital? I think I heard he was taken to Lawndale General . . . ."

By the time he appeared again, she had drained the mug and was feeling warm and mellow. It was hard to suppress a squeal of glee when he said, "Afraid I have bad news."

"Oh?" She pursed her lips and held her breath.

"He's in intensive care."

"I knew that, you idiot!"

"You knew it?"

She backpedaled. "I mean—he was severely beaten, wasn't he? Where else would he be but in intensive care?"

"Well, you were right. He survived brain surgery, but his condition is critical. Usually what they have to worry about is brain swelling. He probably doesn't have a very good chance."

He leaned over the bed and stared into her face. "Your eyes are shining and your cheeks are red. Must be the fever. I'd better do as Mrs. Mendel suggested. Got an ice bag?"

"In the bathroom cabinet." She could scarcely conceal her relief. Or her pounding heart. "Do you really think he might die?"

He answered from the bathroom. "How should I know? Maybe he'll regain consciousness long enough to describe his attacker . . . How well do you know the guy, anyway?"

"What's that supposed to mean?" she snapped.

He gave her a curious look as he passed through the bedroom with the ice bag. "Not implying that you were having an affair, that's for sure."

"Now there's an absurd thought!" she called after him, forcing a laugh. "Our relationship was strictly business. Nothing . . . intimate about it."

"Is," he said.

"What?"

"Your relationship is strictly business. Don't put the poor bastard in his grave before he's dead." She heard him open the refrigerator.

Maybe things would work out, after all. Teddy might not ever come out of the anesthesia, in which case, his crime would never be solved. "Pity," she said under her breath.

He brought in the ice bag and plopped it onto her head, none too gently. "What's with all the pizza in the freezer? And the empty pizza box on the cabinet? You just finished reminding me how you loathe even the idea of pizza."

Her thoughts thrashed about, searching for excuses, but she could think of nothing to say. How careless of her not to have thrown the smaller box into the trash chute last night. He sat on the edge of the bed in a most proprietary manner; she was scandalized to have a man sitting on her bed, but still speechless. Holding the ice bag up with one hand, she pretended to be busy drinking, trying to conjure how Aunt Jesse would react in her situation. She shuddered and quickly thrust that thought away.

"And another thing," he said. "Mrs. Mendel said you wore a gingham shirt last night, and you didn't refute it. What exactly did you do after that church supper?"

She sucked in her breath, but managed to laugh. "Don't be ridiculous! I went to bed."

"You said you went to bed, but your car wasn't here. You went out with someone, didn't you? You had a late date."

"Absurd!"

Norris' voice rose. "It's because of the movie, isn't it? The dirty movie. You were revolted that I took you to it and you've found someone else, haven't you?" His thin face was pinched with pain, and the pale eyes grew pink-rimmed and watery.

"Of course not." But yes, maybe, if she needed an alibi, she could invent a lover . . . except that it would seriously damage her reputation.

"It's that preacher, isn't it? But I warn you, preachers can be as randy as anyone else . . ."

"Norris, stop this! There is no man, I tell you."

The telephone's ring was a welcome relief. She reached for it, but his hand shot out, grabbing it first. Despite everything, the forceful gesture shot a thrill surging through her.

As he answered, then listened, his complexion went from wan to grey to an angry flush. He handed the receiver to Vickie with a cold blame-laden glare.

"It's a man. Someone named Roscoe. Who is Roscoe, Vickie?"

12

There is universal justice. If she ever doubted, she did no longer. And Officer Roscoe Payne, waiting on the other end of the line, was the vehicle to bring it about.

At least, that's what she realized when she came to her senses—after that first heart-stopping moment when she wondered if he was calling to confront her with her crime. But policemen didn't do that. They came bursting through your door, threw you against the wall and handcuffed you while they read your rights.

No, Roscoe believed that she had information. She was sure of it. She wiped her sweaty palm on the sheet and took the receiver.

"We've picked up a suspect in Teddy's beating," he said. "Problem is, Teddy's in no condition to finger him. Sonja says you might be able to identify him as the man you heard threaten Teddy for messing with his ex-girl friend. That's a real break. So I'd like you to come down here and pick him out of a lineup."

While Norris hovered irritatingly close-by, she stalled, trying to decide what to do. She would never have concocted the story she told Sonja had she known that Teddy had survived. She tried to sound enthusiastic. "That was quick! What brilliant police work."

"Lucky break. But I had motivation. I've known Teddy a long time. We started P.S. Twenty-seven together in the first grade."

"Uh . . . how is he?"

"Not good. He may not make it through the night. In that case, we'll have a murder suspect on our hands."

She squelched the sigh of relief. "So when did you want me to do this?"

"Soon as you can get here."

"I don't know . . . I'm not feeling very well . . . I left work early . . . ."

"Look, Vickie, I can't hold this fish for very long. I'd like to get him in a lineup before somebody springs him."

She glanced up at Norris who continued to eye her with suspicion. "There would be no danger to me, would there? I'll be behind a one-way glass?"

"Right."

She cupped a hand over the mouthpiece and turned to Norris. "Could you take me to the police station? It's not the sort of place a woman should go alone . . . I feel duty-bound to help them apprehend Teddy Caplock's killer."

"He died?"

"Well, no, not yet." *But if there is justice in this world, that sex-crazed monster will croak by morning.*

The trip to the jail would serve a dual purpose of proving to Norris that Roscoe and she were not even friends, and she would help to see that sex offender Carl—who had *mooned* her at the park while he was in that undressed state—was brought to justice. Even if it wasn't for the crime he actually committed. Well, what goes around comes around. The circularity of the outworkings of justice was truly divine; what more proof did she need of the rightness of her beliefs?

Norris picked up the soup mug without another word and took it to the kitchen while she finished her conversation with Roscoe. As she ran a comb through her hair, she heard water running in the kitchen sink, then Norris started for the front door to return Mrs. Mendel's mug.

She called, "Don't get caught in one of her long conversations."

But he was still captured at the old woman's door when Vickie came out into the hall. He looked up in obvious relief. "Ah, you're ready to go." He made a great show of looking at his watch and added, "We'd better take the stairs, if you're up to it. Faster than waiting for the elevator."

They fled toward the stairwell while Mrs. Mendel called, "My hot toddy seems to have worked miracles."

Norris still had questions during the drive to the station house. "So how are you involved in all this?" he asked. Norris always drove with both hands on the wheel at the ten and two o'clock positions, they way they teach in Driver's Ed. He made constant tiny little jerky course corrections of the wheel, as if the street were a crooked maze. It was one of his many prissy habits that drove her wild, and tonight, on top of the toddy, it made her queasy.

"I'm not involved. I'm just doing Teddy a favor, you might say: identifying someone who recently threatened him in my presence."

He looked around sharply. "Where? At work?"

"No . . . On the street. I happened to run into them one time."

"Were you with Teddy?"

"Heavens no! Watch the road!"

"Did you go out with him last night, after the church supper? Is that who you went to meet?"

There was just enough truth in his supposition to give rise to panic and cause her voice to sound shrill despite her best intentions. "Certainly not! Now get off this subject and pay attention to where you're going. And talk about something else."

But he preferred silence, apparently. He retreated into a pout that lasted until they reached the police station parking lot, but Vickie was too distracted by her own thoughts to care. But it occurred to her that it was to her advantage for Roscoe to see her loving relationship with Norris, so on the way inside, she said, "Please don't sulk. It doesn't become you. There is no other man in my life, and you know it."

He pulled the station house door open with a jerk. "What about the one you're going camping with?"

She stopped in her tracks before the open door. "What are you talking about?"

"Well, you're certainly not going alone. Mrs. Mendel said you went out yesterday and bought a bunch of camping equipment. You never said a word about going camping to me."

She forced a laugh as she stepped across the threshold, so that she didn't have to face him. "Oh that woman! She must have confused me with the neighbor on her other side. I think she must have Alzheimer's."

Fortunately, Roscoe was waiting in the lobby. Vickie introduced the two, hoping it was obvious to Norris that she couldn't remember Roscoe's last name; hoping it was obvious to Roscoe that she had a steady beau and couldn't possibly be interested in Teddy. Norris waited in the lobby while Roscoe ushered her to the back of the building and into a viewing booth.

Roscoe said, "We'll have to get serious and take your deposition later, but I'm taking no chances that our man will get sprung before we have an I.D."

Still she demurred. "I'm not sure how this will help."

"It's psychological as much as anything at this point," Roscoe said. He seemed completely self-assured, as only an expert can be.

As the seven men filed in, Vickie panicked. For the first time she wasn't sure she could recognize the man called Carl. Three or four of them were about the same size and build. If only she could see their bare backsides.

"Take your time," Roscoe said, then he barked out some orders over the mike.

"Is one of them named Carl?" she asked.

"I'm not at liberty to say at this time."

She studied the faces of the three most likely prospects. "Could you have those three say something?"

"What would you like them to say?"

"Well . . . how about 'Doris'?"

"Just 'Doris'?"

"Three times: 'Doris, Doris, Doris.'"

As Roscoe instructed the men, Vickie watched their expressions carefully. Only number six registered surprise at the name Doris. But after they spoke, she was still undecided. When Roscoe had them turn around, she thought number two's butt looked more familiar.

Roscoe said, "Anything else?"

"Could you have numbers two and six talk some more?"

"Sure. What would you like them to say?"

"'I must've left them on my bike.'"

Roscoe looked perplexed but gave the instruction. At once number six's eyes widened in what she took to be vague recollection. Unconsciously he glanced down at his right hand, then covered it with his left. But not before she saw the skinned knuckles.

Even before they spoke, she was sure number six was Carl, but she waited until she heard them say the words. "That's Carl, I'm certain of it," she said. "Ask him what happened to his hand. Ask him if he hit Teddy. Make him take a lie detector test."

Roscoe laughed. "Whoa. Who's the investigator here?" He patted her on the back, edging her out of the booth.

"I'm sorry. I'm just so anxious to see Teddy's murderer brought to justice."

"So am I . . . although he isn't a murderer yet. You'll be around all week?"

Good lord, was he coming onto her?

He added, "We'll need a statement, when you're feeling better."

Stay calm, Vickie. You're not a suspect.

"About me hearing Carl threaten Teddy, you mean."

"Yeah. Just in case we can't get an I.D. from Teddy. Your statement might be crucial."

As they walked out to meet Norris, she turned to shake hands formally with Roscoe, just to show Norris how proper their relationship was. Then Roscoe shook Norris's hand.

Norris said, "By the way, what's to keep this fellow from going up to the hospital to finish the job on Caplock?"

"We have a guard on the door. I had to pull rabbits out of a hat to get that kind of V.I.P. treatment for Teddy, short-handed as we are."

"How nice," Vickie said. *Rats! That shoots Plan B.*

As they turned to go, Vickie heard Roscoe's beeper, saw him pull out his cell phone. *Maybe it's good news,* she thought.

They were headed for the parking lot when Roscoe raced past and grinned at them. "Great news. Teddy's regained consciousness!"

13

She was getting used to going without sleep, after the second night. Who could sleep, knowing that Teddy had regained consciousness? Or had Roscoe merely told her that to trick her into making a move that would incriminate her?

Not that it mattered whether or not she slept: She needed the time to plan, to pack. The trick was to be ready, both at home and at the office, in the event her number came up. In case the police came. If Teddy talked.

She planned all night. Toward dawn, she made a meticulous survey of her options and chose the few most versatile items of clothing that would fit into her picnic basket—mustn't give a hint to anyone, especially that gabby Mrs. Mendel, that she might be skipping out. She would store the basket permanently in the trunk of her car, just in case.

She even left her bed unmade, her breakfast dishes on the table, and her trash can full, should the police obtain a search warrant. There must be no indication at all that she had left for good.

Besides, she had a plan for an item in that garbage can, a little insurance policy, so to speak. A gift from God, she might almost say.

But then, she might not have to leave. That's why she must go to work as usual, maintain a facade of innocence. But she would keep in touch with Sonja, who would know what Roscoe had learned from Teddy. In the unlikely event that Teddy was coherent and had identified Vickie to Roscoe, Sonja would be the first to know.

Even if Sonja didn't confide in her, Vickie could tell just by looking at her. If the news was bad, Vickie could simply saunter out as if heading for the restrooms, hit the side exit and take the stairs, and run to her car, parked not in the parking garage as usual, but out on the street where no one would think to look. She rehearsed it thoroughly as she got ready for work.

Not that she believed there was the remotest chance that Teddy would ever be rational again. She knew what nobody else knew: She knew what Teddy's brains had looked like when she finished with him. Even though it had been very dark—the location chosen for that very reason—she had seen his brains glisten in the park's streetlight. No, that couldn't have been wishful thinking. She had seen the blood, strangely black in the nighttime. Teddy was definitely done for.

Nevertheless, she would be permanently prepared to run, and to do that, she would have to leave for work early every day, so as to find a spot to park on the street headed in the direction of the freeway.

As Vickie anticipated, Mrs. Mendel appeared while she waited, picnic basket over her arm, for the elevator. Vickie grimaced. The old bat must rush to her peephole every time she heard a sound in the hallway.

Mrs. Mendel stuck her head out the door just enough for Vickie to see the pink foam rollers on top beneath the hairnet. "Is this the day for the camping trip? I see you have your picnic hamper."

"Not actually," Vickie said, favoring Mrs. Mendel with a cheery smile. "A friend is borrowing it for a family outing."

"That's too bad. Just as you'll be needing it yourself . . . When is your camping trip, by the way?"

"I'm afraid there isn't going to be one after all." Before Mrs. Mendel could pry any further, Vickie, shifting to Alternate Plan B, brightened as if she had just thought of something. "Say! I'm in the mood to bake. What's your favorite pie?"

Mrs. Mendel pursed her lips and frowned. "Oh I never eat pie anymore. Cake either. Sweets are pretty much out for me. When Mr. Mendel was alive, I used to make—"

"Cookies, then. How about a raisin cookie?"

"I never cared for raisins, myself. About the only sweet I tolerate anymore is a carrot muffin."

"I like them, too."

"A miniature carrot muffin with just the hint of a lemon glaze."

Miniature. All the better. As she stepped on the elevator, she waved and said, "Then save room for a muffin tonight. If all goes well, you shall have it."

"Just one?"

Yes, just one, you old biddy. We have to be sure you eat the right one, don't we? Now where to get a small carrot muffin, short of making one?

As she hoped, she arrived downtown ahead of the throng of office workers and was able to find a parking space at the curb a half-block from her building.

Another advantage to arriving to work early was that she could dawdle at the coffee bar and soak up the gossip from the caffeine hounds. The usual crowd, minus Sonja, was already gathered. Good grief, they must sleep there. Sonja made her appearance shortly thereafter, and Vickie could tell that she was bursting with news.

"Guess what! Teddy finally regained consciousness."

Vickie joined the others who quickly gathered around and, taking her cues from them, managed to say, "Wonderful!" with a modicum of forced enthusiasm.

Fielding said, "How is he?"

"Not good. Roscoe said he was too loopy to talk. But Teddy did recognize Roscoe at least." Sonja turned to Vickie and confided in a low tone, "Roscoe got a copy of the mug shot of the guy you identified last night. He's going to take it to the hospital today to see if he can get Teddy to blink in recognition or something."

Vickie's spirits rose. A blink of recognition: that's all she needed. Surely Teddy would recognize the man who had hit him in the jaw. All he needed to do was blink, and then he could die. She left the group and went to her cubicle with a bounce to her step, fired with renewed optimism. She might actually get some work done, after all.

But first she must locate a bakery. She flipped through the yellow pages, then called two before she found one that had miniature carrot muffins. Fortunately, it was within walking distance of the office, if she hoofed it fast. She didn't want to have to move her car and give up the good parking space.

At lunchtime she left twenty minutes early and hurried to the bakery, where she bought eight muffins, all they had left. It would be no trouble to pick up powdered sugar and lemon juice on the way home. Thank goodness for the glaze: it would hide the Secret Ingredient. A shiver of excitement ran through her at the thought of it.

She was so engrossed in her plans that she didn't notice Roscoe and Sonja until they almost collided at the revolving doors leading to the office building. In a momentary panic, she glanced at both of his hands and saw no handcuffs waiting. Good lord. She must be more observant from now on. If he had been coming to arrest her, she would have been a goner.

There was nothing to do but make the best of it. She backed up to allow them to pass, grinning and saying to Roscoe, "Taking your best girl to lunch?"

The couple paused on the sidewalk, apparently in no hurry. Roscoe said, "I'm going to try, if I don't get a call."

Vickie couldn't miss the opportunity to ask, "So how's Teddy? Seen him today?"

"Just came from there. He's holding his own. The nurse rattled off something about his vital signs that was a bit ambiguous."

"But he will pull through, won't he?"

"Hard to say."

Sonja put in, "Teddy didn't seem to recognize the picture of the man—"

Roscoe shot her a look and she shut up. Vickie, still forcing a smile, glanced from one to the other, searching for clues.

She said, "But that doesn't mean Carl's not a suspect, does it? I mean, you can still charge him without—"

Roscoe waved her off. "Ah, we've already let him go."

Stunned, she tried to digest it. "But the girl—that Doris: the one whose clothes they found. She could verify that—"

"Frankly," he said, "I had my doubts about them anyway. The girl never did strike me as intelligent enough."

To cover her paralysis, she laughed. "It takes intelligence to hit someone over the head?"

He studied her curiously and she wondered if she had said too much. But he continued in another vein that threw her off guard again.

"I was referring to the woman Doris," he said. "I didn't figure she was the type to have read the Kama Sutra, and I was right. She'd never heard of it."

The vein at her throat pulsed; she could feel it, and she reached up to cover it with her free hand. "Afraid you lost me there," she said in a feeble voice.

"Seems someone left him an e-mail message setting the time and place of the meeting. It's still on his screen. Had a reference to the Kama Sutra." He looked deep into her eyes. "You know the Kama Sutra?"

"Never heard of it." She managed not to stammer. Before he could say anything else, she turned and pushed on through the doors, stumbled directly to the first floor restroom and threw up.

For the remainder of the afternoon she tried to think what to do. After her heart stopped fluttering, she decided there was still plenty of time. So long as Teddy didn't talk, she was safe. There was no proof to link her to his beating. Nothing to prove she wasn't at home in bed when it happened. That is, if she could get Mrs. Mendel off her back. But then, soon Mrs. Mendel would cease to be a problem.

After work she shopped at the grocery store, making certain she left with a bag large enough to hold the bakery sack as well. She had, after all, promised Mrs. Mendel a home-made treat.

She managed to elude her neighbor when she reached the apartment. It was important to gauge the time, so she waited until after supper to begin her project. About seven o'clock, she went to work preparing the muffins. After stirring up a lemon glaze, she put the muffins into the microwave for a quick zap. Meanwhile, she dug into the trash can and retrieved the mayonnaise jar she'd discarded the day before. Yes, there ought to be plenty left in the bottom to treat one small muffin—and a small dose was all she needed.

On one muffin she spread a layer of the rancid mayonnaise, then covered it with lemon glaze. She placed the muffin on a napkin and hurried next door.

When the old woman answered, Vickie thrust the muffin on her and said, "Try this! I made it just for you, because you've been so nice to me. If you like it, I'll bring you some more."

Mrs. Mendel eyed the muffin and attempted a weak smile. "Maybe later, dear. I don't usually—"

"No, you must try it now, before I glaze the rest. I don't want to pour it on all of them if it's too sweet, or too sour." She held the pastry up to Mrs. Mendel's nose and put on her most anxious-to-please look. "I'll be so disappointed if you don't. I hurried home from work just to make it for you."

Grudgingly, the old woman accepted the muffin and took a nibble. Her eyes lit in undisguisable pleasure. "Not bad," she said.

"Eat up," Vickie said. "You haven't had enough to tell."

Dutifully Mrs. Mendel ate the tiny muffin while Vickie watched. When she finished, she took a tissue from her pocket and wiped her fingertips before she pronounced her judgment. "Very nice. A bit sugary, but nice."

"I'll decrease the sugar on the rest and bring them to you in the morning," Vickie said. She rushed back to her apartment, calling out, "Sweet dreams."

She glanced at her watch. Surely by midnight or one A.M., if the mayo did its work, there would be some result. Not a severe one, she hoped; just enough to render the old bat ill enough to be malleable. She went back to the kitchenette and dumped the rest of the glaze—the untainted glaze—on the remaining muffins, feeling better already.

14

The muffin had obviously done its work. Vickie had to knock for an eternity before Mrs. Mendel finally answered the door. Obviously the old woman was hoping that she would give up and go away, but quite obviously Vickie was never going to do that.

When Mrs. Mendel finally opened the door a crack, Vickie greeted her, pert and smiling, all dressed for the office—but wearing low heels for the task ahead—and holding high the plate of muffins. "Good morning, Mrs. Mendel. I just wanted to drop off these other muffins before I go to work."

"Oh, I don't think so, dear. I'm not—"

But of course, she *had* to put the untainted muffins in Mrs. Mendel's apartment, in case there was a police investigation later. And of course she *had* to get inside to use the phone, in case someone thought to check Caller ID. She gave the door a firm push.

"Why Mrs. Mendel! What's wrong? You don't look well at all."

"Just a little upset stomach. Something I ate. It got me up a dozen times during the night, but I'm better now." The old crone was putting up some resistance, leaning her whole puny frame against the door. "Please take those muffins out of my sight. I couldn't possibly—"

"Of course. But it couldn't have been the muffin you ate last night. I had several, and I feel fine." Vickie continued escalating her pressure against the door. "But Mrs. Mendel, you don't look good. I don't think it's indigestion. You'd better let me call your doctor."

"No, I know indigestion when I feel it." But Mrs. Mendel had yielded her tight grip on the knob, and Vickie was able to push her way inside.

She affected a manner of grave concern as she peered down into the old woman's sunken eyes; she actually did look ghastly. "I don't want to alarm you, Mrs. Mendel, but people sometimes mistake heart trouble for indigestion. And at your age—"

"Indigestion is the polite word for what I had," Mrs. Mendel snapped. "People don't mistake a heart attack for the trots!"

Vickie set the muffins down by the door and took Mrs. Mendel by the arm, leading her to the couch. "Oh that's even worse! You have to let me call your doctor."

"Wouldn't do any good. He doesn't make house calls, the old toad! And if he did, I wouldn't let him . . . charge me a bloody fortune, that's what. Anyway, it's too early. He wouldn't be there at this time of day."

That was what Vickie was counting on. She said, "But his nurse would. Maybe she could call him, get him to prescribe something . . . but no: I know the doctor would want to examine you, to be certain it wasn't a heart attack." She leaned forward, assaulted by the old woman's fetid vapors, and patted her emaciated hand. She could almost feel sorry for the old busybody.

But Vickie could tell by the firm set of those flaccid jowls that she hadn't convinced Mrs. Mendel of anything. So she stood and said, "I don't like to be pushy, but I am not going to leave you here like this. I'm going to phone your doctor and at least get some advice. Now where's his number? And where's the phone?"

Without waiting for an answer, she headed for the kitchenette, scooping up the plate of muffins along the way, and placing them prominently on the cabinet. Beside the kitchen wall phone hung a small bulletin board with, as she anticipated, several doctors' phone numbers listed.

She picked the top one and called out, "Is Dr. Jacob your internist?"

"Yes, but I can't go there. It's an atrium building. You have to park in a big garage and walk a long way."

Perfect! That was a detail she had almost overlooked. She dialed the number and spoke in a low voice to the answering service.

"This is Mrs. Sylvia Mendel's neighbor. She had a bad night and has asked me to drop her at the doctor's office on my way to work. So she'll be there about eight-thirty."

The cool detached voice on the line said, "This is the answering service. You'll have to call for an appointment when the office opens."

Vickie cupped her hand around the mouthpiece so that she could raise her voice without being overheard. "Listen, and listen carefully. If you don't want to be held responsible for this woman's death, you'd better deliver the message that Mrs. Mendel will be there at eight-thirty!" She hung up before the person could argue.

Summoning an air of great urgency, she put on a concerned frown and rushed into the living room. "The doctor says there's no time to waste. He wants to see you right away! I'll go home and get my purse and drive you down."

"But you have to go to work."

"This is much more important than work!"

Mrs. Mendel looked down at her chenille bathrobe, wrapped carelessly around an old flannel gown. "I can't go like this," she said, feeling of the foam curlers beneath the hairnet.

"Mrs. Mendel, the doctor says it's imperative that you hurry! Oh all right, throw on any old dress. You can comb your hair in the car. No one will see us at this hour, anyway."

The old woman pushed herself stiffly to her feet and tottered off toward the bedroom muttering, "At least I'm putting on clean underdrawers. I don't go anywhere without clean underdrawers."

Just as Vickie was letting herself out of the apartment, the telephone rang. Instinct warned her that she must be the one to answer it. She called out, "I'll get it, Mrs. Mendel. You don't have time to talk on the phone."

She rushed into the kitchen and picked up the receiver. As she expected, it was Dr. Jacob. She detected a tinge of irritation in his tone. Good. He would feel all the more guilty later.

"I just received a call from my answering service, who provided me with this number from Caller ID. Is this Mrs. Mendel?"

"No, this is a friend," Vickie said. "Mrs. Mendel just left. She wasn't feeling well this morning, and she asked her neighbor to drop her at your office on her way to work."

"Can you catch them?" Dr. Jacob said. "If she's that ill, she should probably go to the hospital emergency room."

"I'm afraid it's too late to catch them," Vickie said. "Anyway, Mrs. Mendel is hard to dissuade when she makes up her mind."

Dr. Jacob let out an exasperated sigh. "I'm not even due at my office until ten. But I'll alert the nurse. That's the best I can do, for someone who shows up without an appointment."

Vickie allowed herself the ultimate luxury of sarcasm. "Well, I'll tell her that next time, she must be sure not to get ill unless she has an appointment first! That is, if there is a next time for the poor old thing!"

She decided it was a good time to hang up.

She called out to Mrs. Mendel, "That was the doctor again. He said to bring a pillow and quilt. He said you should lie down on the back seat and not sit up for anything!"

She rushed back to her apartment and grabbed up her big red patent purse, into which she had already packed a large plastic garbage bag. Then she returned to Mrs. Mendel's and solicitously led her, laden with purse and her Ben-Gay sodden quilt and pillow, onto the elevator. On the way down, she got specific directions to Dr. Jacob's office.

Once they reached her car in the apartment parking area, she took her time planting the old woman's arms under the quilt in the back seat, verifying again directions to Doctor Jacob's office, watching all the while for her chance—when there was no one else around. And thanking her lucky stars that she'd had the good sense to have her car windows tinted. Then, when the area seemed quiet, she got into the back and knelt on the floor, closing the door. God, the liniment fumes were suffocating! She would have to air the car out for a week after this.

Mrs. Mendel raised her head from the greasy pillow and stared at Vickie in surprise. Vickie smiled and reached into her red purse with both hands, closing them on each end of the plastic bag.

"Just lie back and close your eyes. The doctor told me something to do to help you feel better on the way." With that, she leaped up onto the old woman and slapped the plastic bag over her face with stifling force. *The Lord must be providing me the strength to do this.*

The frail woman struggled mightily to free her arms from the quilt, but Vickie's knees were clamped tightly against them. She was surprised at Mrs. Mendel's wiry strength; it was all she could do to keep that wildly convulsing head from breaking free of the bag. The struggle to maintain control left her panting. But she knew when the battle was won: the body beneath her went limp and almost immediately let out a ghastly sulfurous odor. Vickie, trying to avoid taking in the fetid fumes, took shallow breaths while she held on for a good five minutes more, until her arms and legs began to tremble from the effort. Then she climbed over the seat and started the car, shuddering so hard she could hardly keep her foot on the accelerator.

On her way to Dr. Jacob's, she glanced at her watch, and, pleased with her own punctuality, pulled into a service station to get rid of the bag. She left the motor running and, in case someone was watching, called loudly into the back seat, "Now, don't get up, dear. No, we're not there yet. I'm just going to throw away this trash."

But her performance was wasted on the Pakistani attendant in the pay booth, who never even looked up.

As she pulled away from the station, a tremendous relief washed over her. Now, even if the rest of her scheme didn't work as planned, at least no one could prove she had smothered the old crow with a plastic bag.

She got out her cell phone and called the office. No one would be in yet, which was the way she wanted it. She wanted to leave a message on Trish's voice mail.

"This is Vickie. It's almost eight-thirty, and I'm calling to say I'll be a little late. My next-door neighbor is critically ill and I'm dropping her at the doctor's office." She turned her head and called, "What's that, Mrs. Mendel? No, I'm not speeding." Into the phone she mumbled, "Back seat driver."

The rest of her plan was going to work even better than she'd anticipated; she could tell as soon as she drove into the parking garage and saw a custodian sweeping the floor. She parked as near to him as she could get, then jumped out and opened the back door on the far side, away from the man, jabbering loudly the whole time.

"No, dear, you must let me help you. Here, give me your purse. Now take my arm." She reached in and pulled the limp corpse out by the arms, hoisting it up and dragging it along several feet away from the car, into the center of the garage.

Then, with the body of Mrs. Mendel propped up as erect as she could manage, she stopped and called to the man. "Mister, can you help me, please? I think this woman is too weak to walk much farther."

The custodian, fortunately a large burly man, dropped his push broom and trotted to her aid, catching the sagging body and scooping her up in his arms. Vickie continued to talk to Mrs. Mendel, running along beside the custodian as he strode toward the building's entrance.

"It's all right, dear. The nice man will carry you the rest of the way to Dr. Jacob's office." She patted Mrs. Mendel's lifeless arm and leaned near her head, as if listening. "No, I don't think you could walk that far by yourself."

The custodian glanced over his shoulder toward the reserved parking area. "Dr. Jacob's not here yet," he said.

"But he knows we're coming," Vickie said. "I talked to him this morning. He's alerted his nurse to expect Mrs. Mendel." She hurried to open the door for him, then ran ahead and punched the elevator button.

As they rode to the second floor, she looked at her watch and said, "Oh my gosh, I'll be late for work!" When the elevator doors opened, she bustled ahead, looking frantically for the right door. When she found it, she beckoned to the custodian and handed him Mrs. Mendel's purse while she opened the door leading into the waiting room. Perfect. "Look, Mrs. Mendel's friend is following us to take her home, but I need to go on. Just lie her down on that couch and punch that button to let the nurse know she's there."

The custodian looked dubious. "Okay, but you're sure she's expected?"

"Oh yes! I spoke to the doctor myself."

She patted Mrs. Mendel's arm, which had been swinging freely in time to his stride. "You don't mind if I go on, do you, dear? You know how mad the boss gets." She looked up at the custodian. "She's nodding. It's okay with her." She forced herself to lean over and peck the lifeless cheek. "Now don't flirt with this nice man. Shut your eyes and go to sleep until the nurse calls you."

The elevator doors were still standing open. She hurried to reenter and watched while the custodian disappeared into Dr. Jacob's office with what remained of Sylvia Mendel.

"Take good care of my friend," she called.

"No problem," the man said.

He'd said it: no problem. She hoped he was prophetic. The elevator doors closed on Vickie's greatest problem, and this had been so easy. She felt like celebrating by drinking something wicked. Instead, she whispered, "*Thank you, Jesus.*"

Now if keeping Norris off the track proved to be just as simple, she was home free. And, to use the custodian's words, Norris would be no problem.

15

Roscoe picked up Sonja for lunch again, setting off alarms for Vickie. Before Teddy's beating, she hadn't seen the policeman more than a half-dozen times in all these years. Now he seemed to pop up all too frequently. So she made it a point to be at the lobby newsstand to intercept them when the couple returned.

They were late getting back, which meant that she, too, would be late for the second time in the same day. When they came through the revolving door, she allowed them to pass before she fell in behind. As they paused in front of the elevators, she pushed past several others waiting and stepped up beside them, feigning surprise.

"Well! Lunch together again! This must be getting serious."

Roscoe, like a trapped animal, cast an uneasy glance down at Sonja. "I just happened to need some information from Russ, so Sonja offered to buy me lunch."

Vickie searched from one to the other, hoping for a clue about what sort of information Roscoe was digging for, but both wore bland, noncommittal expressions. She decided to risk appearing nosy and said, "Information about Teddy, I suppose."

The elevator doors opened and the crowd surged forward. Vickie was almost elbowed away from the couple, but it probably wouldn't matter; Roscoe wouldn't talk about the case in front of strangers. So she waited until they had started upward and inched close enough to ask, "How's he doing? Any better?"

Roscoe answered with only a lift of his shoulders; she hoped that was good news—for her. He said no more until they reached their floor. After they had stepped off the elevator, Roscoe said, "Hey, would like to go with Sonja to see Teddy after work?"

Sonja's head snapped around so fast and she shot him such a startled look that Vickie wondered if Roscoe's proposal came as a complete surprise to her. She thought it safe to ask, "But why us? I thought only the immediate family—"

"They'll let you in on my say-so. I figured as the two who were closest to Teddy—I mean, Sonja and I have double-dated with him occasionally, and you . . . well, apparently Teddy confided in you more than anyone else. I thought maybe the sight of a couple of pretty women might be good for him. But if there's some reason you don't want to . . ."

"Oh no!" She tried to think how an innocent person would behave. If she refused to go, it might look suspicious. In fact, she needed to get the lay of the place, in case she had to go back and pull a plug later: finish the job she'd started in Falcon Park. "I get a little squeamish around hospitals. But if you think our visit would do any good . . ."

Sonja's eyes had not left Roscoe's face. Vickie could think of no good reason to linger, so she opened the office door and said, "Guess I'll see you later, at the hospital."

Sonja said, "Want to go home and let me pick you up?"

"No! I—have something to do later." In case Teddy was conscious, in case he implicated her with the smallest look, she wanted to be prepared to run.

Anyway, she had no intention of facing Teddy in the presence of either Roscoe or Sonja. She spent the rest of the afternoon figuring out how to avoid them.

At the end of the day, she stepped to Sonja's cubicle, to find her putting a fresh coat on her already overdone face. "I've got to stay and finish my work, so you and Roscoe go on in to see Teddy without me. I'll try to stop by later, if Roscoe will leave word with the guard or the nurse."

Sonja screwed her mascara into its case and batted heavy lashes, looking disappointed. Something about the purse of her greasy red lips put Vickie on alert. "Can't you table your work until tomorrow?"

"I don't think so. I was really late this morning . . . had to take my neighbor to the doctor. She was—she's an old lady, and really sick. I couldn't get her to hurry."

She returned to her cubicle, smiling at her recent triumph: she had almost forgotten about Mrs. Mendel and that obnoxious Dr. Jacob, who probably had some explaining to do as to why his patient died while cooling her heels for more than an hour in his waiting room. She had to congratulate herself. If only every problem were as easily solved as was the Mendel one. Her only regret was that no one would ever know of her brilliantly executed scheme. Maybe someday she would write a story about it, labeling it fiction.

She took her time about leaving the office, making sure that Russ was aware that she, conscientious employee that she was, had put in overtime to make up for her morning tardiness. Downstairs, she dawdled at the newsstand before strolling leisurely to her car, then drove toward home as slowly as traffic would allow. She decided to stop by the apartment to see if news of Mrs. Mendel's demise had reached the tenants. At every stop light, she practiced a look of shocked disbelief in her rear view mirror.

But the apartment elevator was empty and so was the third floor hallway. Disappointed by the lack of activity, on a whim she stepped up to Mrs. Mendel's door to knock. Checking on her health would be a nice touch, in case anyone was listening. But—

It could have been her imagination, but from inside Mrs. Mendel's apartment, she thought she heard a muffled scrape, as of someone scuffing a shoe against the floor. Hair rose and prickled the back of her head, and she walked quickly to her own door and scrambled to get it open, heart thudding.

Once securely locked inside, she moved cautiously to the wall adjoining Mrs. Mendel's and put her ear to it, fantasizing that somehow the old bat had been resuscitated by Dr. Jacob or else had risen from the dead. Even now she waiting until Vickie eventually knocked—and then she would fling open the door, and—

She heard nothing . . . or did she? Was that a wheeze, or the fourth floor plumbing? It could be that Mrs. Mendel's next-of-kin had been notified, whoever that might be, and they were already there, pawing through her belongings like vultures.

It might even be the police. Maybe a tenant had seen her this morning in the back seat with Mrs. Mendel—someone she failed to notice in the shadows of the car port. Maybe they didn't realize what they saw until the old woman's death was reported, then they called the authorities—

The telephone jarred her nerves. She jumped and gasped, then, relieved for the distraction, rushed to answer, controlling her quick breaths as best she could. The sound of Norris' nerdy voice was, for a change, a welcome one. But almost immediately her relief changed to exasperation; Norris' calls were becoming far too frequent. What right had he to call on an ordinary weekday?

"Now what do you want?" she snapped.

"I thought we might—take our relationship to the next level," he said tentatively.

Her heart thumped. "What's that supposed to mean?"

"Go out to dinner on a week night."

Was that all? She smirked; Norris had no class at all. *Now, Teddy would have . . .*

The thought—where had it come from?—stopped her cold and brought a return to her self-control. She said, "I'm sorry. I'm busy."

After the briefest pause, he blurted, "I knew it! You're seeing somebody else on the side. It's that preacher, I bet."

A light bulb went off: so that was what this "taking the relationship to a new level" was about: Norris was checking up on her. Her lip curled in disgust. "You don't want to take me to dinner; you're just jealous! And for no reason. I don't have a date—"

She froze. Again the scuffing noise coming from next door. She pressed her elbows against her sides to stop the shivers, swallowed, and said, "I'm going to the hospital, if you must know, and I was just about to ask you to come along."

"To see your friend Teddy? I get it! He's the one!"

Scrape. Scrape.

Now she was terrified of even stepping into the darkening hallway. She was not above wheedling. "Norris, if we are ever going to 'get to the next level," we'll have to trust each other. I want you to go with me to the hospital . . . I'm afraid!"

"Afraid? Of what?"

"Of that terrible man who did this, the one they had me identify in the line-up-and then they let him go. What if he's out to get me? Norris, I need a man! A real man."

She let this soak in, then, afraid she may have spread it on too thick, may have scared the weasly little twerp off completely, she added, "Anyway, when you see Teddy and me together, you'll see there could never be anything between us."

"Oh? Why's that?"

"Teddy is too crude. Not anything like you." She crooned the last line; she could almost have set it to music. And it worked.

His pleasure was disgustingly transparent. "Not like me, how?"

From somewhere in her archetypal bag of feminine tricks, she pulled out a coy husky purr. "You know . . . appealing, in a non-threatening way." She paused and dared to add a word she'd never used in her life: "Sexy."

Norris was easily persuaded from that point, and she even convinced him to come upstairs to her door for her. That solved the immediate problem, but she wondered if she would ever again feel safe leaving her apartment, without risking facing the specter of Mrs. Mendel.

When she hung up, she tiptoed to the wall to listen. Almost certainly there was somebody inside, but whoever it was must be deliberately trying to keep quiet. If only she could flush them out. Then inspiration struck: she would ask Norris to check on the old woman. Meanwhile, she remained crouched against the wall, hearing for the first time every tap, every pipe gurgle, every flush in the entire building.

Norris was thirty minutes away, but somehow he made it in twenty-five, flushed and walking with an odd gate, as if something were out of place in his hinter regions. She opened the door only a crack, barring the entrance into her front room, and said, "I'm almost ready, but I promised Mrs. Mendel I'd look in on her this evening. Could you knock and tell her I'll be by later?"

Like a dutiful child, he stumped next door while Vickie cowered out of sight, listening. His knock set off a ruckus inside Mrs. Mendel's apartment that took only a moment to identify: a wildly yapping, racing, scratching, frantic little dog!

Vickie came into the hall. "Oh my lord. The old crone was keeping a pet. Wait'll the manager finds out."

Norris frowned down at her. "She's a lonely old woman. Surely you're not going to turn her in."

She thought about the poor little guy, stuck inside with no food, no water, maybe. How long before someone rescued him? She said evenly, "Mrs. Mendel was ill this morning. Maybe the dog is trying to tell us something; maybe she's too sick to come to the door. I think we ought at least to alert the manager on our way out."

Again he scowled. "I don't want to be responsible for getting her in trouble. What if he made her move? No, we'd better stay out of this."

Reluctantly she locked her door and whipped around, stalking toward the elevator without glancing his way. Norris was a stubborn ass. And a jealous fornicator. And a nosy bastard. *He'd better watch his step.*

16

They followed the arrows to Trauma Intensive Care, past ambling armies of green-clad stethoscope-strung personnel, all of whom seemed to be on break. Vickie muttered, "Doesn't anybody work in this place?"

She glanced at the chrome wall clock, noted that it read six o'clock, and figured the strollers were heading for supper. A few workers were wheeling multi-tiered carts down the hall filled with trays of aluminum-covered dishes. Some of it actually smelled appetizing.

Norris said with a note of hope, "Maybe we could stop off in the cafeteria on the way out."

She grimaced at the irony. "Somehow I presumed the 'new level' of our relationship would be upward."

They had no trouble locating Teddy's room: it was the only one on the Trauma Unit with a guard at the door. Vickie approached him timidly and identified herself. He nodded in recognition, but looked past her to Norris and said, "Sorry, buddy, you'll have to wait out here. Roscoe didn't say anything about you. Anyway, only one visitor's allowed in at a time."

Vickie breathed in relief: she had managed to elude Sonja and Roscoe. She cast a glance back at Norris that promised a speedy return and pushed into the room. Except for one small night light and a blipping monitor screen, it was dark.

The unidentifiable head-swathed figure lay inert in the bed, strung with a lacework of tubes pumping life into it. As if she might wake him, she crept soundlessly up to the bed, not certain, now that she had a closer look, that it was really Teddy. The blackened eyes, the purplish stain down one temple—had she actually caused that? A respirator tube distorted the mouth, and she wondered if Teddy's new bridgework was lurking in a nearby drawer, or if he had had implants; it didn't look like Teddy's smirking mouth. Portions of his arms had been shaved, and they were bruised from needle punctures. Even the backs of his hands were fastened to tubes. The hands—were those Teddy's hands? Maybe he was still out there somewhere, sending secret messages.

Tentatively, she whispered, "Teddy? Can you hear me?" It seemed to her that his eyelids twitched, but they didn't open.

Her gaze was captured by a bump in the covers about midway down, and she gasped in horror at his audacity. Even in this condition, he dared to display that despicable erection. The sight fed her fury, and she came to an immediate decision: Teddy must be eliminated, once and for all.

But how?

She moved to the far side of the bed, studying the apparatus that was keeping him alive. If she unplugged it long enough to dry up his brain completely—but wouldn't the monitor alert the nursing staff? There must be something else she could do . . .

She knelt down to study the wall plug—and caught a glimpse under the bed of a man's shoe in the far shadows of the room. At first she presumed it to be Teddy's shoe, until it moved. Heart bounding, she straightened quickly and squinted into the dim light, her eyes now becoming accustomed to the dark. Someone was sitting in a chair behind the door.

It was a set-up.

A man's voice said, "Looking for something?"

Her whole body fluttered, but she thought fast. "I—had—I was wearing a—bracelet when I left home. I've just discovered it's missing."

The man rose and shuffled into the light: the rawboned crags of Roscoe's face cast menacing shadows. Her knees threatened to fold, but she thrust out her chin and eyed him steadily. He looked down at the corpse-like patient and boomed, "Teddy? Look who's here: Vickie."

At the sudden sound of the loud voice, the hooded eyes popped open and darted from Roscoe on one side of the bed to Vickie on the other, fastening on her such a terrible glare that there could be no doubt: Teddy knew.

But did Roscoe know? Was that wild accusing stare as evident to the policeman as it was to her? She steadied herself against the edge of the mattress and did her best to smile, playing the scene of her life, at the same time wondering how she managed to allow herself to let Roscoe get between her and the only door to escape.

"Teddy! It's me! I'm so glad to see you awake." She squeezed his cold fingers, then forced herself to lean over and kiss his whiskery cheek. It was her second death kiss of the day, and Teddy didn't smell any better than

Mrs. Mendel. She would have to scour out her mouth before she could ever eat again—providing she got out of this room in one piece. She was vaguely aware that her kiss caused an escalation of activity on the monitor.

The door flew open to admit a sturdy bustling nurse, who pushed Roscoe aside and whipped out her stethoscope. As she bent over Teddy, she snapped, "Clear the room! His vitals are going berserk!"

As they hurried out the door, the nurse called, "I thought I stipulated there was to be only one visitor at a time!"

"I was just taking a cat-nap," Roscoe said lamely. When they had passed the guard, he turned to Vickie and added, "I haven't had much sleep lately. Thought it wouldn't hurt to catch a few winks in Teddy's recliner."

She was breathing easier now. So it hadn't been an ambush after all. She looked around for Norris and saw him pacing vacantly outside the waiting room down the hall. He waved, then frowned as Roscoe fell in beside her to walk down to meet him.

Acting was becoming second nature; she found it easy to sound contrite. "I'm sorry our visit was cut short. I wanted to talk to Teddy. He seemed more alert than I'd been led to believe."

"It's hard to know," Roscoe said. "He didn't respond at all when Sonja was here."

"The nurse was obviously angry. I hope we didn't upset Teddy . . . cause him to have a relapse."

As they approached the still scowling Norris, Roscoe said, "I don't think so. Too bad you didn't have a chance to look for your bracelet. I'll ask the nurse to check around." He held out his hand to Norris.

Norris shook hands, reluctantly it seemed, then turned to Vickie. "What's this about a bracelet? I thought you hated wearing jewelry."

"I do," Vickie said quickly. "That's why I kept opening and closing the clasp. Unconsciously I was probably trying to lose it."

Norris's face was contorted with suspicion. "What kind of bracelet was it? I don't remember you having on a bracelet."

"Maybe it fell off in the car," she said, taking his elbow, pushing him along.

But Roscoe wouldn't be left behind. He quickened his pace to match—even overtake—theirs, saying, "Keep your eyes on the floor. You could have dropped it on your way in."

Norris persisted with the stubbornness of a jackass. "Which arm was it on? I think I would have noticed it when we were trying to rouse old Mrs. Mendel—"

Roscoe, whose long legs had placed him several strides ahead, stopped. His head snapped around. "Mendel? An old woman?"

Vickie couldn't make her dry tongue work, but Norris had become disgustingly loquacious. "Vickie's next door neighbor. We were trying to get her to answer the door."

Roscoe resumed walking, his features drawn in a thoughtful moue, a rough-hewn version of a Rodin. "That name showed up on some list at the station this afternoon. I'm trying to remember . . ."

Vickie broke in. "I really am worried about that bracelet. Norris, can't you hurry any faster?"

She caught his hand and forced him to break into a trot, which this time Roscoe did not attempt to match. He seemed still lost in a deep ponder, his great frame hunched over in thought. She and Norris waved goodbye as the elevator doors opened, but he didn't look up.

On the way down, all the way home, Norris would not let the subject go. "I don't remember any bracelet. Are you sure you were wearing one?"

Finally she burst out, "Norris, will you stop it with the bracelet? All right! Maybe I was mistaken. Maybe I didn't have it on. Now can we just drop it?"

He glanced over at her in mock surprise. "Why Vickie! What's wrong? You were the one who was so anxious to get to the car to see about your bracelet, and then you hardly looked . . ."

His sarcasm wasn't lost on Vickie. "All right. What's eating you this time?"

"Oh sure. Always my fault, isn't it? Blame the victim, that's your game."

"What are you talking about, Norris? How in God's name are you a victim?"

"This whole trip was a rendezvous for you and Roscoe, any fool could see that. When he saw me, he just made up the thing about the bracelet to explain his presence there."

Vickie ground her nails into her palms. Norris was becoming insufferable. What could she ever have seen in the spineless twerp? Again she reined in her emotions and tried to answer rationally. "That's absurd. But I should have been more thoughtful of you, explained how Roscoe happened to be there. It's just that I-I'm so worried. Roscoe saw Mrs. Mendel's name on some list. What if it's on the morgue list? What if she's died?"

"Mendel's a common name. Just because her dog is barking is no reason to think—Anyway, the morgue? Isn't that a little dramatic?"

"Don't be peckish," she said. "If there's anything I can't stand, it's when you niggle over every little thing." There. She hadn't meant to say anything. Far better to pretend acquiescence. But Norris would try the patience of Mother Teresa. There was just so much she could stand.

By the time they reached her apartment, they had sullenly abandoned dinner plans. At her insistence, Norris walked her to her door. There were no sounds from next door, so Vickie presumed the manager had been summoned by some other tenant and the offending pooch had been removed. Good. There had been no ghosts, and now there was no dog. And she had seen with her own eyes Teddy's broken body safely tucked into a hospital bed. She could sleep peacefully, for a change.

But unbidden came the vision of the rising staub beneath the covers, just as she fumbled for her key and slammed it into the lock. The memory almost unnerved her completely, caused her actual contractions in her gut. Involuntarily, her hand flew to cover her mouth. She felt violated by the mere thought of the awful thing.

In Norris's present sulky mood, Vickie did not need to offer him her cheek for a goodnight kiss. She mumbled her thanks and slipped inside, locking the door securely behind her. For a few long moments she leaned against it, breathing hard, listening as the elevator doors opened and closed.

Finally she gathered her gumption and swept through the small apartment flipping on lights, then she switched on the television full blast. Maybe she would poach an egg and watch a sit-com or two, just to take the edge off. She went into the kitchenette to boil some water when the unmistakable whir cut into a second's silence from the tube. The sound sent her in to her desk.

"Now who would be sending me—?" she muttered, picking up a single sheet which at first appeared blank.

But not quite.

On it were written two words:

"*Tsk. Tsk.*"

17

It didn't take a rocket scientist to figure out that, on his way home, Norris must've stopped at the all-night copy shop and sent the fax. Norris was so predictable. "Tsk tsk" sounded just like him. She could almost hear him say it, jutting out that bony chin in disapproval.

In time, she would have to deal with Norris, but now something else was more pressing: Teddy was lying in ICU with a hard-on, and his eyes flew open at the mention of her name. She would have to finish him off, and do it soon, before he regained his power of speech.

No plan presented itself until the next morning, when she got into her car with the intention of getting to work a half-hour early. She noticed Mrs. Mendel's pillow and quilt in the rear seat and thought, *Of course*. The old broad could help her out, after all. She gathered them up and headed back into the building to the super's apartment.

Art Reuther was not known for his charm. He opened his door wearing half-zipped twill pants and an undershirt that revealed breasts bigger than hers and a pendulous tub where his abs ought to be. He hadn't shaved, and his bottle-red hair with grey roots hadn't seen a comb in a while—or a shampoo, for that matter.

She forced an urgency into her tone that she hoped Reuther would translate as concern; actually, she was in something of a hurry. She didn't want to be late for work again.

"Sorry to bother you so early, Mr. R., but Mrs. Mendel left these in my car yesterday when I dropped her off at the doctor's office. I can't rouse her to return them, and I'm worried that something may be wrong. Will you come up and open her door?"

His ruddy, veined features drew together in a frown as he said slowly, "Come to think of it, I figured she wasn't home last night when I went up to see about the dog."

She pretended ignorance. "Dog? In our building?"

He stepped into the corridor and headed for the elevator, with Vickie double-stepping to keep up. "Yeah. Somebody complained about the barking. I don't know how long the old lady's been hiding him. She's probably been carrying him in and out in that shopping bag she always has with her. This time, I figured she went out and left him behind and . . ."

On the ride up to Three, she asked, "Uh—what did you do with the dog?"

He shrugged with no sign of remorse. "What could I do? Pets are against the rules. I tossed him out the front door. Cute little pooch. Somebody probably picked him up."

Poor creature, she thought. *But then, dogs have no souls.*

They stepped off the elevator and Vickie fidgeted with growing impatience while Reuther went through the formality of knocking and waiting before he unlocked the door.

Once inside the apartment, a mirror image of hers, she called out, "Mrs. Mendel? Are you here?"

As Reuther started for the bedroom, she caught his arm. "You'd better let me go in there alone. She might have fallen in the tub." She pointed to the kitchenette. "You look in there."

She hurried through the bedroom, which was redolent with lingering fumes of Vicks and Ben-gay, the bed a tumble of fusty bedclothes grey from wear, and rushed for the adjoining bathroom with a purpose. She would have probably only about twenty seconds before Reuther followed. A mesh baby gate with a hole chewed through it barred the way, but she quickly climbed over, narrowly missing a pile of dog dung. Surely the medicine cabinet would have something she could use. *Help me, Lord.*

As she rummaged frantically through the shelves of pill bottles, several clattered into the sink. She heard Reuther call, "Everything okay in there?"

Still she fumbled at the bottles, reading labels. "Everything's a big mess in here," she answered. "Looks like this is where she kept the dog."

He stuck his head around the door jamb, red-rimmed eyes narrowed in curiosity. "What're you doing in here?"

"She left a big mess of bottles scattered everywhere. I'm just trying to put them back into the medicine cabinet." Defeated, she scooped the vials out of the sink and began setting them on the glass shelves.

Reuther glared at the floor in distaste. "She's gonna have to clean up this crap in a hurry. This is why we don't allow pets in this building. Some people live like animals, y'know?"

Vickie sighed and climbed back over the barrier, eyes raking the bedroom. Surely somewhere in this apartment there was a bottle of sleeping pills.

Then she spotted them on the bed table, beside the half-filled water carafe. She couldn't read the label from this far away, but the bold-face "Warning!" at the bottom was clearly visible. She thought fast.

"You know, her doctor's telephone number must be around here somewhere . . . Did you notice any kind of bulletin board in her kitchen—something with phone numbers on it?"

Dully he shook his head. "Nope. Nothing like that in there."

Men! "Are you sure?" she snapped. "Go look again."

As soon as he stumped away, she ran to the bed table and picked up the bottle. As she hoped, it was sleeping pills. She slipped them into her pocket and returned to the front room to wait for Reuther.

After he had discovered the bulletin board beside the wall phone—*how could he have missed it before, the doofus?*—and jotted down the number, they left the apartment. Vickie turned aside to her own door and said, "Would you mind phoning the doctor? I'm already late for work."

She left him grousing that this was not in his job description, entered her apartment and went straight to the kitchen tool drawer. She poured the sleeping pills onto the bread board and, using a hammer, beat them into a powder, as fine as she could get it. Then using the side of her hand, she carefully brushed the powder back into the bottle. She carried it to the sink and dripped a cautious amount of water into the bottle, shaking the contents to be sure the powder was dissolving. Then she returned it to her jacket pocket.

Before she left the apartment, she had another inspiration: she stopped by the bedroom and rummaged through the meager contents of her jewelry box until she came up with a small gold link bracelet, which she slipped into the other jacket pocket. A glance at her watch satisfied her that she still had time for a brief stop at the corner pharmacy near her office to purchase a syringe. She selected one with the largest needle she could find, so that any chunks of undissolved powder would pass through.

Now all would go smoothly if Roscoe followed his recent pattern and took Sonja to lunch, so Vickie could be sure that he wouldn't turn up at the hospital during the noon hour.

Morning at the office seemed to drag interminably. She finished folding several reports, putting them into envelopes, and typing up their labels, making this small chore last most of two hours. Each time Sonja left her cubicle, Vickie stopped her work to follow. Once, at the coffee bar, she managed to ask, "Is Roscoe picking you up for lunch again today?"

Sonja looked surprised. "Why? Do you want to see him about something?"

"No!" She sounded a bit too emphatic. "Just—making conversation.... You have been having lunch with him pretty regularly."

Sonja shrugged and stuck her face into her mug. So much for that. Vickie tried again.

"Anyway, I was just wondering if we might have lunch together sometime." As Sonja glanced up in astonishment, Vickie hurried to add, "But not today. I've got to run an errand for a friend from my apartment."

She turned away and walked up toward Russ's office. The suspense was too much. Maybe she would go on to the hospital and just risk Roscoe showing up. Russ's door stood ajar, so she ignored Trish, sitting at her desk supposedly screening his visitors, and stuck her head inside.

"I have to run by the drug store for my neighbor on the noon hour. All right if I leave a few minutes early?"

Russ didn't look up, but said, "Yeah, yeah. We're running a freakin' delivery service here anyway."

She returned to her cubicle to get the all-important jacket, now containing the syringe as well, and went into the rest room. There she shut herself in a toilet stall, took out the syringe and filled it with the sleeping mixture. As she left the rest room, she knew fate was with her, because Roscoe and Sonja stood waiting for the elevator. She greeted them almost jubilantly.

Roscoe said, "You seem to be in a good mood. Did you find your bracelet?"

"Huh?" Dear me. What to say. "No, but maybe if I have time, I'll stop by the hospital and ask the nurse is anyone has turned it in."

Sonja said, "So what's the urgent errand you have to run for your neighbor?"

The errand. "Oh. Actually, I'm going by to ask her doctor what happened to her. Nobody's seen her since she went to see him yesterday." She was babbling. Saying much too much. Why couldn't she stop?

She was grateful when Fielding and Jennifer pushed into the elevator just before the doors closed. She pretended to be shoved over, allowing the newcomers to stand between her and Roscoe and Sonja. When the doors opened on the ground floor, she waited discretely in back until the couples had left, then she lingered at the lobby newsstand until they went through the revolving doors. Anyway, she had to get rid of the pill bottle. As she left the building, she walked to the curb and tossed it into the storm drain, smiling in satisfaction as she heard it clatter onto the concrete far below.

On the drive to the hospital she rehearsed her speech, so that when she arrived, she approached the guard with just the right degree of urgency and disappointment. He was leaning against the wall outside Teddy's door, munching on a sandwich as she rushed up.

"Oh dear!" she said with a wail of dismay. "You're not the same one who was on duty last night!"

The guard swallowed a bite and said, "No, that's Bob. He comes on at three."

"Roscoe let me go in to see Teddy Caplock last night, but I dropped my bracelet while I was there. The nurse made us leave before we had a chance to look for it . . . You wouldn't let me go in and look for it now, I suppose."

He shook his head. "Sorry, lady. I just can't do that."

She had an inspiration. "Not even if you go in with me?"

He looked dubious, but she could tell he was weakening. "Well . . . I don't know . . ."

"It'll only take a minute. It's a bracelet that belonged to my grandmother. It's not worth much, but I'm afraid if the cleaning help finds it, I won't get it back. Oh please go in with me." She tried her best to quiver her chin and squeeze out a tear.

In obvious alarm that she might succeed, he said, "Okay. But only for a minute."

He opened the door and, without so much as a glance at Teddy, she hurried to the bed's far side and knelt on the floor, out of the guard's view. Quietly she slipped the bracelet from her pocket and, coughing loudly to mask the noise, sent it skittering across the floor beneath the monitor table. Then she said, "Oh! I see it! But I can't reach it! Can you get it for me?"

As he approached the far side and knelt down, she rushed to the other side of the bed, where Teddy's intravenous feeding bag hung. There was no time to open the bag's top; she simply poked a needle hole into the plastic bag above the level of the liquid, and with one swift plunge, sent the sleeping potion into the bag. Good. There was a large enough knock-out punch in his feeding to stop Conan the Barbarian.

But before she could return the syringe to her pocket, the guard popped up from the other side of the bed, bracelet in hand. "You were right!" he said, handing it across the bed to her. She thrust the syringe behind her, balling it in her fist and crying out at the sudden pain: she had rammed the needle through her thumb. Tears sprang immediately to her eyes as she managed to reach for the bracelet with the other hand.

The guard looked concerned. "Gosh! It must've really been a special bracelet to make you cry like that."

She tucked the bracelet in her pocket and turned her back, pretending to look for a hankie, while she extricated her thumb from its skewer. Blood gushed, and she rammed hand and syringe into her pocket and turned back to face him, allowing the tears to course freely down her cheeks.

"It's not the bracelet," she said. "It's poor Teddy here."

For the first time she glanced down at the patient—and gasped. Teddy's wide-eyed glare bore into her again as if to say, I know what you did. Her heart thumped and crashed against her chest. She was terrified that he might speak at any minute.

Pressing her forefinger against the throbbing thumb to stop the bleeding—God, what must all that blood be doing to the inside of her jacket?—she thanked the guard and hurried away. If she got out of there fast, maybe he wouldn't even think to tell Roscoe that she'd come.

On the way back to her car in the parking lot, she found a trash bin, where she disposed of the syringe. Now there was nothing to tie her to Teddy's demise. He would simply stop breathing and that was that. In her car, she found an old tissue in the glove box and made a bandage of sorts for her thumb. It would have to be her right thumb; she did everything with that thumb, even steer the car. She would have to drive with her damn thumb sticking up in the air.

Suddenly she was ravenously hungry. She drove through the Oinker and got a double ham sandwich and a big root beer to go. She ate with her left hand, while she drove with four fingers.

Back at her office, she stopped in the rest room, washed away the blood, and bought a bandage from the vending machine. The thumb still hurt, but pain was a small price to pay. As she returned to her cubicle, she was almost giddy with relief, until Russ stopped by and asked, "Get your errand run so soon?"

"Huh?" She stared at him dumbly until she remembered. "Wouldn't you know? The doctor's office was closed at the noon hour. I'll have to take care of it after work."

He looked puzzled. "Doctor's office?"

Oops. Wrong story. "The drug store needed to phone to verify the prescription," she said, congratulating herself on her quick thinking.

He stared at her chest, frowning. Good lord, men were such animals. What was there about her that brought out the lust in them? But he said, "Is that blood on your blouse?"

She looked down at the unmistakable stain and said, "No! It must be catsup."

"Doesn't look like catsup to me."

"Well it is. It's a secret sauce they have at the Oinker. That's where I had lunch."

"The Oinker way over on Thirty-fourth? What were you doing over there?"

She stammered. "Did I say the Oinker? I-I don't mean the Oinker . . . I can't remember the name of the place. It's—just around the corner . . . You know the place." Before she made any more mistakes, she waved him off and turned on her computer to check her e-mail.

And let out a muffled shriek of terror.

On her screen she read:

I know what you did. Naughty girl.

18

It had to be Norris. After the first surge of unreasoning panic subsided, she knew for a certainty that Norris had sent the message. He had followed her again. The little weasel must be spending his every lunch hour stalking her, trying to catch her in a tryst with somebody—Roscoe was apparently his current suspect. Norris must've been lurking outside Teddy's hospital room just now, expecting to apprehend her in a compromising position, when he inadvertently witnessed her putting the sleeping mixture into Teddy's feeding bag.

Why hadn't he confronted her then? His motive seemed clear enough: He didn't care a fig whether or not she finished Teddy off. All he wanted was leverage, something to hold over her head to blackmail her into doing his bidding. Becoming his love slave, most likely. Or something even more vile.

She gripped her fists, seething with fury against Norris Griswold for spoiling her beautifully crafted plan. Now she would be forced either to deal with Norris, who would be very wary—

Or marry him. So he couldn't testify against her.

She shuddered at the mere thought.

"Vickie? Are you all right?"

Startled, she looked up at Russ, still standing at the entrance to her cubicle. Even as he spoke, before she could react, he stepped inside and peered over her shoulder at the monitor.

"Oh thank God," he said. "From the look on your face, I thought your hard disk had crashed, or else you'd made a fatal miscalculation on the Pantheon account." He squinted at the screen. "Hmm. 'Naughty girl.' You haven't miscalculated it, have you?"

With shaking fingers she switched off her e-mail and called up the Pantheon spread sheets. "Of course not! See? Here are my original projections, and here . . ."

As soon as his concerns were mollified, his tone became imperious. "I take it, then, that was a personal message?"

She answered hastily, calling up indignation with no effort. "Another of the unsolicited ones I've been complaining to you about."

His scraggly eyebrows raised in mock surprise. "Oh? I thought you told me Teddy was responsible for those." Was Russ making fun of her?

"I thought so originally. But Teddy and I cleared that up, long before his accident. We were on the best of terms by then. In fact, he was trying to help me find out who's responsible." Might as well take advantage of a bad situation, since there was no chance now of Teddy ever contradicting her.

She shifted so as to steal a quick glance at the wall clock, figuring that the contents of the bag must surely have dripped through the tube by now and saturated Teddy's body, so that soon he would be history. A slithery glob of inert flesh, already beginning to rot. She smiled a wicked little grin as she swung around to find Russ studying her quizzically.

He raised his hands and said, "I won't ask whether that look means that you admit to being naughty, because I don't want to be accused of sexual harassment."

As he backed out of her cubicle, eyes twinkling with mischief, a stunned Vickie watched him go. She sucked in her breath and held it. Russ had used those two words in the same sentence: naughty and sexual. How dare he? A looming cloud of doubt hovered overhead. Could it be that she had dismissed Russ as a suspect prematurely?

But she was getting off the track. All evidence, albeit circumstantial, pointed to Norris. Norris could not keep on dogging her, thinking his lascivious thoughts, taking her to pornographic movies that showed naked, glistening bodies . . . waiting to pounce down her blouse again and touch her nipple with his bare—but no! No. That was not it . . . Now what was it? Oh yes: Norris must be silenced before he talked, before he told anyone about what she'd done to Teddy. She picked up the phone and called his office. Although he was coolly formal, Norris could not hide the surprise and, she detected, mild pleasure at her call. This was no time for posturing or pride on her part. She plunged in.

"I thought you'd like to know that Teddy's guard found my bracelet. It had slipped under the monitor table. So you see, there really was a bracelet. And I really wasn't just looking for an excuse to see Roscoe."

"Oh." He sounded more disappointed than contrite. "Well . . . I guess I owe you an apology."

"No you don't," she purred. "If anything, I owe you one. I didn't take you seriously when you suggested raising our relationship to a new level." She paused for effect, evoking the ancestral genes of feminine wiles to produce a husky breathiness she didn't know she had in her. "I guess I was afraid to hope that you really meant it."

There was a perceptible pause. Good. She had rendered him speechless. This was actually quite simple. Finally he cleared his throat and said, "Of-of course I meant it."

Ah. She could reel him in. She whispered, "Can't we start over with the new level? I have some creative ideas of my own."

His tone was pregnant with doubt. "Like what, exactly?"

She produced an unVickie-like giggle. "Telling would ruin the surprise. Why don't I pick you up at your place tonight at nine?"

"So late? And why my place? I always pick you up."

"This is to give you time to shower first . . . and put on clean underwear."

As he choked and sputtered, she added, "Oh dear. I hope I haven't given too much away . . ."

She got off the line quickly to leave him stewing in his juices while she put her mind to formulating a plan for Norris's extinction. She had none at this point, but she always thought more creatively when her back was against the wall.

But by five o'clock she still hadn't come up with a plan.

God, maybe it would be easier just to marry him, she thought grimly as she drove into her apartment parking stall. She couldn't put him permanently to sleep; she'd already used Mrs. Mendel's entire supply. She hadn't seen anything else in the old woman's medicine cabinet . . . .

But maybe she could look again, if she could think of another excuse to get inside.

Of course. By now, Mr. Reuther would have phoned the doctor and learned of Mrs. Mendel's demise, and helpful Vickie could offer to go up to her neighbor's apartment and search in her address book so as to notify next-of-kin.

She stopped at the super's apartment and knocked. When he opened the door, allowing billows of cigar smoke to escape, she noticed that Mr. Reuther hadn't bothered to change since this morning. But allowing her gaze to travel downward, she was relieved to note that at least sometime during the day he had at least managed to get his trousers zipped all the way up. He frowned in irritation. Behind him, the television blared, and she could see a beer can on the floor beside his recliner. She smiled her most fetching and apologized for the interruption.

"Did you reach Mrs. Mendel's doctor? Did he tell you what happened to her?"

"Yeah, yeah. Like we figured, she didn't come home that day."

"Oh?" She cocked her head, fixing him with wide expectant eyes. Even managing to flutter her lids a bit.

"Naw. Won't be back for several days, most likely. Maybe a couple of weeks. Good thing I sacked that pooch when I did."

Her jaw was literally locked at half-open. He looked at her for a moment, shrugged, then started to close the door. But he thought better of it and opened it again long enough to say, "She had some kind of spell at the doctor's office. The nurse even had to perform CPR. If you want to go see her, she's over at the hospital in intensive care."

19

Completely numbed, Vickie let herself into her apartment. There must be some mistake, she was certain. The old woman wasn't breathing—unless somehow, the janitor's jostling had started everything working again. Even so, how could she have survived? Wouldn't her brain have been so starved for oxygen that she would be unable to remember anything about Vickie's attack? Yes, surely that would be the case.

But she had to go see for herself. She glanced at her watch. Still almost three hours before she was due to pick up Norris. She had planned to spend the time in the calm silence of her apartment, working out a foolproof plan to remove Norris from her life. But how could she think about Norris with Mrs. Mendel lying up there in the hospital—possibly in the same bed formerly occupied by Teddy—spouting off accusations about being suffocated?

She drank a small glass of buttermilk, but even that didn't set well. No matter: it would be impossible to digest anything until this new problem was solved. If only she had access to more sleeping pills—but no, she must be more creative than that.

No need to get in a dither until she found out what went so terribly wrong with her beautifully executed snuffing out of the old bat's life. She grabbed up her purse and left the apartment without even checking her messages.

At the hospital there was little need to stop at the information desk; she knew very well where intensive care was located. She went directly to the fourth floor, then realized that she didn't know the room number. Reluctant to have her face recognized—*in case there's an investigation later*, she told the watching semi-circle—she put on her sun glasses, stepped to the nurses' station, and asked for Mrs. Mendel's room.

The nurse frowned over the top of her glasses and asked, "Are you the niece?"

Vickie feigned surprise. "Oh, is my sister already here?"

"Well, somebody's here, but she doesn't resemble you."

"Oh? What does she look like?"

"A flashy brunette with a leopard coat."

"Must be my cousin," Vickie said lamely. "Uh . . . the room number?"

"Four-seventeen. No visiting except by immediate family at the specified hours."

"I guess we're as 'immediate' as Aunt Sylvia has . . . Is my cousin in the waiting room?"

"Probably. You can't both go in at once. You'll have to decide between yourselves."

Vickie hurried off to the waiting room and easily spotted Mrs. Mendel's niece sitting well away from the other waiters, eyeing them with distaste. A woman of heroically-disguised middle years, she had thrown the leopard-skin coat over the back of her chair. Her sleek black hair had been bushed and coiffed to within an inch of its life. She wore a black pants suit, spike heels, and an emerald ring the size of a horse. Vickie went in and sat demurely beside her, but the woman shifted to the far side of her seat. Vickie stuck out her hand, which the woman ignored.

"You must be Mrs. Mendel's niece—I've forgotten your name. I'm your aunt's neighbor and dearest friend."

The woman gave a stiff smile through bright red lips pumped full of collagen. "Oh. Glad to know you. I'm Barbra Kline." But she folded her arms across her chest to avoid shaking Vickie's hand.

"How—how is—Sylvia?"

The woman shrugged. "Hard to say. She's a little delirious right now. Keeps grabbing the nurses and trying to convince them somebody tried to choke her."

"Choke her? Mercy! Why?"

"Seems she had some kind of spell at the doctor's office and the nurse there gave her CPR. Probably saved her life. But Aunt Sylvia has it in her mind that the woman was trying to kill her."

Vickie could hear her heart thumping, so she rose and pretended to pace with anxiety. "How terrible! Does this mean she's lost her mind?"

"I dunno. The doctor says she may snap out of it. The old girl's made of iron. Nothing'll ever kill her, I'm convinced. I'm the only kin she has. She's been a burden to me for years."

Vickie managed to look disapproving. "But your poor aunt . . ." She altered her expression to one of hopefulness. "So does that mean that she's going to survive?"

"Undoubtedly," Barbra Kline said. She looked up. "I'm sorry. I didn't get your name."

As Vickie was casting about for an alias, she heard a man's voice behind her, coming from the doorway. "Vickie? Is that you?"

Surprised, she wheeled around at the unmistakable sound of the policeman's voice. "Roscoe! What are you doing here?"

He stepped inside the waiting room and sauntered over. "I usually visit Teddy at this time of the evening; you know that." He nodded toward Barbra, who was now sitting more than erect; she had thrown her silicone chest out so far, she threatened to topple from her chair head-first.

Roscoe smiled. "Is this someone new from the office?"

"No. This is Barbra Kline. She's here to see someone else."

Barbra extended a brilliant long-nailed claw languidly and cooed, "Pleased to meet you."

"Roscoe—."

He turned back to Vickie. "But why are you here? You know Teddy still can't have visitors without my say-so."

Vickie sucked in her breath. Could it be possible that Roscoe did not yet know? She said, "I just dropped by to . . . see how he's doing."

Barbra Kline was not to be ignored. "Oho! I thought you came by to see how Aunt Sylvia is. Or maybe you just dropped by because of the handsome policeman." She batted her Estee Lauder-thick lashes at him. "Can't say as I blame you."

Roscoe colored, ducked his head and actually began scuffing his toes against the tile floor. Vickie thought she might puke. But he recovered his composure abruptly and said, "Teddy's much better. This afternoon he had a real break-through. He actually reached over and yanked the tube out of his arm! The nurse didn't discover it until the whole bag had run out onto the floor, but despite that, his fluid levels remained stable. There's a possibility his condition may be upgraded after the doctor comes by."

Vickie felt her hair turning white from the roots out. Teddy, that turkey, had saved himself! If he regained his speech—or even if he was able to communicate by writing—she was doomed.

Roscoe was saying, "So who is Sylvia?"

"A neighbor," she mumbled, anxious to escape. She looked at her watch. "I've got a date."

"With Norris?"

"No!" God, what a mistake. Later, when the body was found, it would seem as though she intimated that she was the last to see Norris alive. She stammered, "It—it's not that kind of date. I . . . have to see . . . my . . . my pastor. About . . . some . . . things . . ."

She fled with a wave and frenzied goodbyes flung over her shoulder, wondering how in the world she would ever get out of this mess. And she still didn't even know how she was going to deal with Norris. She'd have to pray about it.

20

With no notion which problem to attack first in her agitated state, Vickie sped out of the hospital parking lot and headed toward home. Dispensing with Norris no longer seemed so urgent. Teddy's miraculous rally meant that she was either going to have to do him in quickly or else leave town and be on the run for the rest of his life.

Damn Teddy Caplock! Why was he so hard to kill?

And old Mrs. Mendel! Who would ever dream she could be so resilient? If the old witch regained consciousness, regardless of what happened to Teddy, Vickie would still have to flee.

She glanced in the rear view mirror and saw with alarm that Roscoe's squad car had followed hers out of the parking lot and now was directly behind her. She would know that silhouette anywhere: he was so tall that his head brushed the headliner. An icy chill convulsed her whole body. Did he know? Had Teddy somehow already conveyed to him what she had done to his feeding bag? Maybe Roscoe was simply playing cat and mouse with her back there in the hospital waiting room. But for what purpose?

There could be only one purpose that she could think of: blackmail. He would toy with her, threaten to bring her to justice unless she did exactly what he wanted. She could readily imagine what that would be. What did every man want? She couldn't bring herself even to think about it.

She shuddered and forced her attention to the street ahead. She was probably being ridiculous. Roscoe knew nothing. She would have sensed it back at the hospital if he knew.

But what had she told him? That she was going to see her pastor. Unless she could shake the policeman, she would have to stop at St. Timothy's rectory, which wasn't such a bad idea, now that she considered it. Roscoe would have to drive on by and leave her alone. If instead he parked at the curb down the street, she would know for certain that he was actually tailing her.

She touched her left turn signal and felt another cold shock as she saw his direction light flash. He *was* trailing her! As she neared the pastor's manse, she steeled herself to confront Roscoe when they stopped. But when she pulled in at the curb, he gave a couple of beeps in greeting, passed her and waved, then sped up the street. She groaned in relief and wilted back against the seat.

Good. Now she wouldn't have to up to Reverend Clark Wortham's door. She waited a good five minutes to make certain that Roscoe didn't circle the block. She was so intent on watching the traffic behind her through the mirror that she didn't notice someone approaching her car. A tap on the window caused her to jump and let out an involuntary squeal.

But the person bending down to peer quizzically at her was not Roscoe. It was the pastor's housekeeper, Mrs. Twickham. With a great sigh, Vickie rolled down the window.

Mrs. Twickham, a tall gaunt woman of no less than seventy years, smiled a rare smile, revealing a generous mouthful of dark, uneven teeth. "Didn't mean to startle you. I noticed you sitting out here for quite a while."

Vickie swallowed. "I—had just talked myself out of bothering Father Clark about my little problem."

"Oh, he's never bothered by one of his parishioners. Especially a pretty woman who's obviously very upset. But I'm afraid you're out of luck, dear. He's still out on his sick rounds. You're welcome to come in and wait, though."

Perfect. Vickie declined, thanked Mrs. Twickham and said a hurried goodbye, leaving the startled housekeeper still crouched forward at the curb. Time was getting away. All these digressions were not in her schedule. She would have to hurry home to take care of this new emergency.

When she reached her building, she went directly to Art Reuther's apartment. The super opened the door wearing a bath towel and a scowl. Good grief! Was this paunchy beer guzzler trying to seduce her too?

She kept her gaze riveted to his face and feigned obliviousness to his scandalous state of undress. As usual when she was faced with a crisis, the words flowed flawlessly from her lips. "I've just been to the hospital to see Sylvia—"

"Who?"

"Mrs. Mendel. Anyway, she's doing fine, but she wants me to bring her a few things. Would you mind opening her apartment again for me?"

The red-rimmed eyes narrowed in the fat grizzled face. "Oh yeah? Why didn't she just give you her key?"

"She wanted to. But I didn't want the responsibility of having her only one." The excuse sounded lame, even to her. She allowed her gaze to travel past the bulging belly, with its midstream of vulgar black growth, down to the towel that barely wrapped his girth. "Only I see that I've caught you at a bad time. So if you'll just lend me the key for a minute . . ."

He grumbled and went off to the other room, leaving her standing in the hall, marveling at the kind fate that had brought her to his door at bath time. If Mr. Reuther weren't wearing a towel, he would never have given her the key; he would have accompanied her, which would have made her search of Mrs. Mendel's medicine bottles much more harried.

As soon as he returned with the key, she dashed to the stairwell, too impatient to wait for the lumbering elevator. She arrived at the third floor breathless but with spirits newly buoyed. This time she would not leave Mrs. Mendel's until she had found every single bottle that could possibly be of use. But getting the medicine was only half the battle. How to introduce a lethal dose into both Teddy's and Mrs. Mendel's food without being detected would call for great ingenuity.

She let herself into the old woman's apartment quietly, so as not to alert the neighbors, who might remember this night later. The fetid smell of dog feces now permeated the entire interior, but she shielded her nose and mouth and made straight for the offending bathroom, taking shallow breaths behind her hand. A few bottles still lay in the lavatory and on the floor, in addition to the jumble in the medicine cabinet. There were more, she remembered, on the bed table, and still more, probably, in the kitchen. She spent a lengthy time going through each room, gathering up any bottles that showed promise. Later she would phone a pharmacist and find out which were the most lethal.

Eventually she had collected more than a dozen bottles, including one containing tiny nitroglycerine tablets. In the kitchen broom closet she found a large shopping bag to put them in and, taking one last look around the apartment, she stepped into the hall—and backed into Mr. Reuther, now fully dressed.

Art Reuther had a way of making her feel guilty, anyway, even for a legitimate complaint about a broken heater or a loose faucet. He glowered from her to the bag and back to her. "Well, it's about time! I hadda come all the way up here to find out why you didn't bring back my keys. What took you so long?"

With the back of her hand, she swiped the sudden bead of sweat from her upper lip. Then she handed him the keys, talking fast. "I had a hard time finding what she wanted. Mrs. Mendel never remembers where she put anything." Before he could get a good look at the bag, she swept past him to her own door. "Excuse me. I'm in a terrible hurry. I've got a late date. "

Oops. Shouldn't have said that. What if someone comes around later to investigate Norris's disappearance and Reuther remembers . . . but no, he never pays attention to anything I say.

As she entered her apartment, she glanced at her watch, stunned to realize how much time she had spent in Mrs. Mendel's. It was already well past eight o'clock. What must Norris think? She was the soul of punctuality, as he well knew. She would have to phone him immediately, stall him for a half-hour more, think of some excuse. Flat tire, maybe.

The red light on her answering machine indicated a recent call. As she played it back and recognized the grinding petulance of Norris' voice, she grimaced. How she had put up with him this long now seemed incredible.

"It's five after eight." His aggrieved tone suggested that she might have left him at the altar. He sighed heavily. "Since there's no answer, I'll have to presume you're on your way. This was your idea, you know, and it is a week night."

In no mood for a sermon, she flipped off the machine before hearing the rest. She dialed his number and got a busy signal; no doubt he was trying to phone her again, the impatient creep. She left the bag on the desk and ran to the bathroom. Then it was absolutely necessary that she change into something dark and nondescript and do something different with her hair.

In the back of her closet she found an old purple knit turtleneck shift that her mother had sent. She'd never worn it but had saved it in case her mother ever asked about it. Perfect. She faced the imaginary semi-circle of inquisitors to remonstrate: *Someone dressed in purple, you say? Everyone will tell you I never wear purple. Besides, that day I had on a grey suit with a green blouse. Just ask anybody. Roscoe should remember. He saw me about the time the suspect was spotted.*

While she was changing, the doorbell rang, and she cursed aloud. "Norris! He couldn't wait a measly five more minutes?"

She pulled on the dress and grabbed a belt and rushed to the door in her bare feet. It wouldn't do for someone to see Norris standing in her hallway on the same night that he disappears.

But when she threw open the door, it was not Norris who waited, but Father Clark Wortham, grinning disarmingly.

"Father Clark!" There was no way to conceal her obvious dismay at being caught barefooted, although she tried, hiding one set of naked toes under the other set. Somehow it seemed vulgar and unseemly to allow her minister into her living room when she was not fully clothed, but even as she tried to think of a reason not to admit him, he was already advancing across the threshold.

He glanced down, chuckling. "Don't worry. I've seen unclad feet before. You should see how some of my parishioners greet me."

Blushing, she stepped aside and allowed him to walk past, close enough that his woody shaving lotion left a trail under her nostrils. The dark, slightly curly hair on the back of his neck had grown shaggy, something Norris would never allow to happen. The sight sent tremors of excitement through her chest. The man obviously needed care—or was his unkempt state a deliberate ploy to lure her into . . .

He stopped in the middle of the room and stood awkwardly, obviously waiting to be invited to sit. She ignored her own impulse toward courtesy and remained by the door until he said, "I apologize for dropping in unannounced. When I finished my rounds, I phoned my housekeeper to alert her to heat up my supper. She told me you'd come by in a very agitated state. I tried to call, but your line was busy. Since I wasn't far away, I decided to stop over. But I see I've caught you dressing to go out."

"No!" It was amazing how panic sparked her creativity. She managed a grateful smile and moved to the couch, indicating a chair for him. "I've just come home, actually." But would he later remember the purple dress? "How thoughtful of you to come. It was just that—well, I've been worried about my friend Norris Griswold."

He ignored her gesture toward the chair and dropped onto the couch beside her. Hastily, she tucked the naked feet under her.

He said, "Your boy friend?"

"Oh heavens no! He's nothing like that! Except that—well, he's become much more serious about me than I am about him. Recently he asked me to—take our relationship to a new level, and when I refused . . . ."

He interrupted. "New level? Just what does that mean? Sex?"

For a moment she was too shocked to speak. That a minister would speak so openly to her could mean only one thing: Clark Wortham was smitten with her, just like all the rest. He had become a tool of the Devil.

It can happen to anyone. She moved farther into the corner of the couch and said in a voice cold with distaste, "I couldn't possibly know what you are driving at."

An easy smile played across his face. Was he mocking her? "Sorry. I thought 'sex' was a universally understood word. But go on. I've distracted you."

She took a deep breath and composed herself, recapturing the somber mood. "He threatened to kill himself. He accused me of seeing someone else. He was completely irrational, insanely jealous over nothing. I'm afraid he might do something terrible to himself."

The pastor's manner had shifted dramatically. The dark brows knitted in grave concern. "I'm sorry. No wonder you're so overwrought. Would you like me to talk to him?"

"No!" She thought fast. For some reason, the scent of shaving lotion wafted by and with it, inspiration. "That wouldn't do at all! Ever since you came by the other night to return my stole, I'm afraid he's become jealous of you. He suspects you of being my . . . my—"

She had embarrassed them both: the area on either side of his eyes fairly pulsed with color. He cleared his throat and became all business. "I see. Then why exactly did you come to see me this evening?"

"For advice. I wanted to know if you think he's serious."

He nodded. "We should always take a threat of suicide seriously. Do you think you could convince him to seek counseling?"

Before she could answer, the doorbell rang again. The two of them exchanged startled glances before she jumped up to answer it. They both knew who it would be—knew how it would look.

With great reluctance she opened the door to Norris, who glared at her bare toes and then at the pastor, who had leaped to his feet guiltily.

"So!" Norris stalked into the room, chin jutting, pale-fringed eyes blazing. "Now we know. Now we have the reason for your peculiar behavior of late."

She looked helplessly at the pastor, hoping he would speak, but he seemed tongue-tied. His Adam's apple bobbed like a yo-yo behind his cleric's collar. She turned back to Norris and stammered, "I-I don't know what you mean."

Norris spun and fastened a gaze of contempt on her that plainly labeled her as a junk-yard harlot. "You almost had me convinced. Until this moment, I had just about decided that, if you weren't seeing someone else, you must be the woman who's trying to kill Teddy Caplock."

Her mouth went dry and she cast about frantically for the proper retort: something that smacked of outrage. "What—what a sick thing to say," she finally managed. She pointed an imperious finger toward the door but, noting the discolored thumb bandage, lowered her hand and put it behind her. "I think you'd better go."

But the rector brushed hurriedly past her saying, "No! I'm the one who should be going. Mrs. Twickham is waiting supper for me." The brush was no accident. The place where his shoulder touched hers burned with the heat of his desire for her.

He stopped at the door and faced a glaring Norris, but what Clark Wortham said sounded phony, even to Vickie. "You must understand, Griswold, that it is the duty of a minister to visit all of his parishioners. But if my coming here disturbs you, I won't call on Ms. Ledbetter in the future."

With a stiff nod toward Vickie, Wortham left before Norris could answer. As the door closed, Norris turned a questioning gaze to Vickie, who had been planning a convincing reaction. Tears seemed to be the most natural; she didn't even have to fake them.

Shaking, she flopped onto the sofa. "I've never been so mortified in my life!"

Norris seemed too stunned to speak at first; then she heard him take a tentative step forward. He waited while she snuffled grimly on, then finally he said, "I guess I overreacted."

Not looking up, she nodded. The evening had been a disaster. She was too weak, too beaten to talk anymore. All her plans had come to naught, and she was on the brink of being implicated by both Teddy and Mrs. Mendel. What was to become of her? It was all so unfair.

Quietly Norris let himself out the door and closed it, and soon she heard the elevator bell. The finality of the sound galvanized her into action: it was the red-alert. If she was going to push Norris off City Center Bridge, it would have to be tonight. And if there was a chance at all that she might still escape detection, Norris would definitely have to go. Besides, after his performance tonight, Norris needed to go. She leaped up and rushed to throw open the door just as he was entering the elevator.

"Hold up for me while I get some shoes," she called. She rushed in to grab her boots, which she would put on during the trip down. While Norris pouted, no doubt.

But he didn't pout. Instead, he watched in obvious astonishment as she hopped around the elevator, forcing the boots on her bare feet. It was such an unsanitary thing to do; she'd never gone without proper hosiery before. She would probably have blisters in the morning. But there simply was no time for niceties; anyway, imagine pulling on pantyhose in his presence!

"We can't part this way," she said, panting not so much from the exertion as from the realization of a crucial opportunity almost lost.

"What do you have in mind?" The pale brows hunched close together, pulling all his features inward—except that damned pointed chin, which always managed to look commanding, like Roosevelt. He wasn't making it easy. It would be an uphill struggle to regain his trust so as to salvage the evening.

She tried to think of a way to arouse him and began by leaning helplessly against him. But he only staggered backward, almost pitching her off her feet. The elevator's lumbering creaks masked the sound of her fury, which she surely must have made audible. She fought to conceal fresh loathing and spread her lips in what she hoped passed for a coy grin. "I had originally planned something special for tonight. Aren't you the least bit curious?"

By the time they reached the ground floor she could see him softening. The colorless brows had returned to their neutral position above the red-rimmed eyes, which had lost their blatant glint of indictment. Everything might work out after all, if nothing else went wrong.

A young boy was pressing his nose against the glass of the front entrance. When Norris opened the door, Vickie noticed that the boy was holding a small frazzled dog.

"My mom told me I can't keep this dog," he said. "I saw a man throw him out of this building."

Vickie gasped. "Mrs. Mendel's dog!" Without thinking she reached out, but the dog snarled and snapped at her hand, digging his tiny needly fangs into her injured thumb, slicing cleanly through the bandage. She yelped in pain as blood spurted in every direction.

Norris shooed the boy away and with unconcealed distaste ushered Vickie back inside. "You'd better see to that wound. Besides, it's getting late and—"

"But I have something to show you." Even as she spoke he backed out onto the walk.

It was too dark to see the frown that his voice evinced. "Do you think I want all that blood in my car?"

In an instant he was gone, trailed by the boy with his dog. She muttered, "Damn little mongrel! That bastard Norris owes his life to that dog."

For twenty-four hours, at least. But Norris would get his tomorrow night, in spades. By that time she would have dispensed with Teddy and Mrs. Mendel one way or another.

She looked down at the throbbing thumb, now dribbling blood onto her purple dress and her good black boots. Maybe she would do the dog in, too.

21

Pain had kept her awake for hours; the twice-injured thumb was the hammer to the kneecap of an already crippled plan of extermination. But despite the discomfort and dejection of that long night, daylight brought fresh optimism. The dog bite, of course, provided the perfect excuse for missing work. She phone the office before she even got out of bed, then lay back staring at the ceiling trying to order her day.

What a schedule! Victims were stacking up at an alarming rate. By the time the day was over, she would be exhausted. Still, the sheer exhilaration of accomplishment would buoy her.

She got up and went in search of the bag containing Mrs. Mendel's pills. She seemed to recall that nitroglycerine in a large enough dose could be fatal. She could grind up enough to inject into Mrs. Mendel's IV, but if Teddy had been moved from ICU, he probably no longer had an IV. Anyway, she mustn't let herself be seen by Teddy. Somehow she would have to slip something into his food before his tray was delivered to him.

Or better: she would prepare something at home: a treat of some kind, that she could put on his tray just before it was taken into his room. A bon bon, perhaps. A truffle, stuffed with ground nitro. She smiled with the anticipated pleasure of preparing it. She had always loved to be creative in the kitchen. She perched on a high stool and contemplated a bowl of fruit on the bar, mentally making a list.

The day—and evening—would call for new wardrobes. She would need a complete disguise for her visit to the hospital. And before she escorted Norris to City River Bridge, she would change into something new and dark as the night—and inexpensive, since she could never wear it again. Stealth and caution would require that she travel by cab, by an elaborate succession of cabs. The new clothes, the cab fares, it would all tax her pocketbook, but whatever the cost, this day could be the last free day of her life if she wasn't careful. Maybe she would be wiser to spend the money on getting out of town, establishing a new identity—except for the fact that if she retreated, Teddy Caplock would go unpunished for his loathsome messages, and most importantly, for sitting on the edge of her desk and thrusting his crotch at her face.

Her cheeks burned with the shame of it. Her breasts heaved at the perversity. Certain parts of her body broke out in moisture at the outrage of it: that grotesque bulge at eye-level, so close that if he had advanced on her, she would have been helpless— Trembling, she reached for a banana, peeled it and ate it in ravenous gulps, realizing that she must be weak from hunger. One banana didn't satisfy her, and she reached for another but didn't peel it immediately. Instead, she rolled it from side to side, stroking it as she thought.

No, regardless of the risk, she must obliterate Teddy Caplock from the earth. If she failed with Mrs. Mendel again, it would be no great catastrophe; Barbra Kline would happily corroborate her contention that the old bag's accusations were a case of senile dementia run riot, especially if it meant that Sylvia Mendel would be locked away in an old folks' home permanently.

As for Norris, his jealousy, his suspicion, his possessiveness were intolerable. Then there was his uncontrollable lust. She well remembered when he lost control and thrust his craven fingers into her bra. Her skin crawled at the thought of it.

Not quite the same sensation as the reverend's oh-so-subtle brush against her shoulder. Still she had felt his urgency pulsating through their clothing. Clark Wortham, for all his dedication to the body of Christ, still clearly lusted after the body of a woman: her body. To desensitize him, she would have to attend church more often—yes, that would be a wise move, anyway, to allay suspicion as to any part she might have played in the deaths of the others.

But she must take care not to wear a low-cut dress, because as she knelt at the rail to take communion, she might very well incite his passion. And although she ought to continue to sit on the front row, she must never wear a tight skirt, or one that might ride up. The minister had a way of fixing her with his gaze when he was making a point. Sometimes she had known he was staring straight up between her limbs, but his sermon was so mesmerizing, she was powerless to cross them, powerless to move at all.

She put the banana, skin and all, in her mouth and with a savage jerk, ripped off the tip with her teeth.

22

Every move must be carefully considered. She began the day by looking up several addresses in the yellow pages and putting them in her purse. She tightly bandaged her throbbing hand, forced on a pair of gloves to hide the bandage and, dressed in a nondescript denim shirt and jeans, drove to the nearest ATM. There she drew out a substantial sum to be used for purchases and for cab fare, so that, if later there was an investigation into her activities, her movements could not be traced. She chose an odd amount of cash so that, in case her bank account was examined, she could claim she bought a piece of jewelry from a flea market vendor who insisted on cash. An old brooch of her mother's would pass as her purchase, if anyone should ask. *You remember seeing me at the flea market that day*, she rehearsed her ever-present circle of witnesses.

Next she drove to the flea market, parked her car, and walked two blocks to a cab stand. She gave the cabbie the address of a hardware store on the other side of town that happened to be across the street from a wig shop. Such elaborate precaution might not be necessary, but she would take no chances. When she arrived, she went into the hardware store and waited by the front window until the taxi had turned the corner, then she exited and crossed the street.

In the wig shop, she paid cash for a jet black bob with bangs closely resembling Mrs. Mendel's niece Barbra Kline's, and an ash blond shag that was as near to the woman Doris's as she could remember. Anyway, it matched the description she had given Roscoe of Doris's appearance.

To be on the safe side, she wore the black wig and walked four blocks to a discount department store where she bought a pair of sun glasses with purple rims, an enormous pair of gold-plated earrings, bangle bracelets, and a cheap white uniform and white shoes. She also picked out an atrocious leopard-spotted blouse that she would lose no tears about discarding after one wearing. Finally, she bought a wildly multi-colored acrylic cardigan that would be hard to forget.

Her last stop was a large mall, reached again by cab, where she purchased a large shopping bag for her clothing and other wig. She had chosen this particular mall because of its gourmet candy shop. Before she entered the shop, she stopped in the restroom, put on the sun glasses, earrings and bracelets and discarded the wig boxes in the trash receptacle. Glancing at the wall clock, she congratulated herself: only twelve o'clock. Almost five hours left to get ready.

She spoke to the candy store clerk in a high nasal whine that she hoped sounded like Barbra Kline, and picked out the smallest box of truffles she could find, paying for them with a flourish of the bangled hand.

As she left the mall, she stopped in the drugstore for two more large syringes. Then, her purchases completed, she returned to the mall restroom to remove the wig, glasses and jewelry, then phoned for a taxi and returned to the flea market parking lot, where she put the shopping bag in her car trunk.

She drove to the grocery store, where she bought two loaves of bread, two heads of lettuce, and two large bottles of juice, asking the sacker to double-bag them in paper. Back at the car, she removed the bottles from the bags and replaced them with the wigs and clothing, placing the bread and lettuce prominently on top. Then she was ready to return to her apartment.

With her two grocery bags, she rode the elevator up in solitude, her elaborate preparation to camouflage her purchases wasted. But she must still be cautious at every step of the way. As she let herself in the front door, she noted with alarm that her clock showed that it was well past two. How could she have lost so much time?

There was no time to eat lunch. A banana would have to suffice. She had taken to keeping a large bunch on hand at all times.

The next hour was spent filling both syringes with a mixture of nitroglycerine and Evian water, one so thick that it was almost a paste. With great care, she injected the pasty one into the bottom of a truffle, then repeated the process with a second candy, in case the first became mashed in transit. The whole process was time consuming, if one were to do it right.

There was still plenty of time to experiment with several quick make-up tricks that would be easily accomplished in a hospital toilet stall. She carefully packaged the cosmetics into two baggies, one for each costume change, so that she wouldn't waste time groveling in the bag.

Now as to the bag: the shopping mall bag was too obvious. She rummaged in the closet and found an old straw tote that was perfect. She packed her costumes, make-up, truffles, and the one filled syringe into the tote, then frowned. What could she put on top?

In the same closet she found an appropriate box, which she wrapped in a slightly creased piece of gift paper, taping on a used bow that she'd saved since Christmas. Not too professional, but no one would scrutinize it that closely. She placed the gift box on top in the tote and glanced at her watch. Hospital dinner was served early—about 5:30, she had observed. She picked up the tote and prepared to leave when the phone rang.

She groaned at the delay, until she realized that later she might need an alibi to prove her whereabouts. Caller I.D. revealed that the parson was on the line. *All the better*, she thought, as she picked up the receiver.

Clark Wortham's tone was hushed and almost conspiratorial. "I feel obligated to tell you that Norris Griswold is in my study," he said. "Naturally, I consider everything you told me last night as confidential, but in view of the seriousness of the situation—"

"Seriousness?" she said. What had Norris revealed to Clark?

"His threat to commit suicide, of course."

"Oh—yes!" She had completely forgotten what she had told the minister.

"In view of that, I'd like your permission to tell Norris that I know, that you are very concerned—"

"No!" *Dear God, that weasel Norris would ruin everything yet.* With great effort, she brought her voice under control and thought fast. "Norris would lose all trust in me if he knew I told you about his suicide threat."

This was the perfect opportunity to strengthen her alibi for the time when they found Norris floating in City River. Allowing a sob to catch in her throat, she added, "I love Norris very much. I had hoped that someday we would marry."

"What? I thought last night you said Norris was the serious one and you didn't reciprocate his feelings."

"I-I lied!" she said brokenly. "I mean . . . I didn't realize how much he meant to me until last night, when he broke in and found us together. All night I've lain awake crying because I've bungled things so badly . . ."

He sighed. "I understand. In that case, of course I'll keep our talk confidential."

She thought of something else. "But what can Norris want? Do you think he might attack you in a fit of jealousy?"

"It did occur to me," he said.

"Then don't see him! He's very unpredictable."

"That's out of the question. In fact, I mustn't keep him waiting any longer."

"Then phone me back when he leaves." Immediately she regretted saying it. As much as she must know what Norris told Clark, if the minister found her not at home, she would lose her alibi. So she added, "I'll stay right here, close to the phone."

"All right. I'll call, but I'm in an awkward situation now. What Norris tells me will also be privileged."

"Of course. But at least you can let me know that he didn't hit you."

As soon as she hung up, she took the receiver off the hook again and laid it on the desk. Later she would contact Clark and claim that a talkative relative had kept her on the line for hours.

This changed everything. Norris had moved up to the head of the list again. Last-minute changes were so distasteful; she liked order in all things. But flexibility had its place, if one were to be successful in accomplishing goals. She put her cell phone in her purse, picked up her tote bag and left the apartment. With luck, she could still take care of Sylvia Mendel and Teddy Caplock before the evening was over.

In the meantime, she drove to Clark Wortham's street, parked down the block, and waited.

23

It was almost five o'clock. If she didn't get to the hospital by mealtime, she would miss her chance to put the nitro-laced truffle on Teddy's dinner tray. And she would miss her chance to soup up Mrs. Mendel's IV just before visiting hours and the arrival of that bitchy Barbra Kline at her aunt's bedside. The whole operation, including two costume changes, would take less than thirty minutes, but it was a crucial thirty minutes. After six o'clock she would be free.

Free to take care of Norris. Tonight.

But she must wait until dark and until traffic had died down on the old City River Bridge.

A higher level indeed! Vickie was well aware of what that innocent sounding bromide led to. Wasn't she witness to such "higher level" escapades more than once—the first time being thirty years ago? She was barely five when curiosity drove her to spy on her grandfather and her teenage cousin Imelda, who often sat together in the porch swing in the afternoon. Grandfather, who claimed to be offering sage advice about Imelda's future, complained that the late afternoon air was chilling and always covered their knees with a lap robe.

But when Vickie secretly crawled under the swing and peered up through the slats, she saw Imelda's bare bottom and Grandfather's roving fingers. When Imelda's gasps and squeals grew too loud, Grandfather would shush her and raise his own voice to a "higher level": "Of course, you could go to nursing school, marry a rich doctor . . . ," Oftentimes, after these sessions, Grandfather would carry the lap robe into the house, holding it in front of him, and retire to his room, from which he would shortly emerge wearing different trousers and toting his laundry bag. Grandfather always did the wash after he and Imelda had sat together on the porch.

So that was what old men were like: they wanted to touch forbidden places and cause young girls to squeal and shudder. And other men were no different, she had learned as she grew older. Usually they invented some high-flown excuse for what they really planned to do.

But Norris was stupid enough as to warn her what he had in mind, just as Teddy had done with his obscene messages. What was wrong with these ego-centered males? Did they believe a woman would be flattered at their disgusting intentions to deflower her? Vickie crammed her cell phone between her thighs and waited.

At length Norris came out of the manse, got into his car, and drove away. Vickie followed at a prudent distance, noting with relief that he seemed to be heading toward his apartment. Good. He was safe enough for now.

From between her legs her cell phone jingled, sending a mild pulsation into her groin. She pulled into a curbside space and parked before answering, turning on her radio to mask the sounds of traffic.

It was Clark Wortham, sounding more tentative than ever. "I promised to phone you when Norris Griswold left, although there's not much to report," he said. "He certainly doesn't appear suicidal, at least."

"Oh? But what did he want? Is he suspicious of . . . you and me?"

His tone was even more hesitant and noncommittal. "I can safely say that he is not suspicious of me."

Me, he said. Not *us*. What did that mean? Was Norris suspicious of her for reasons other than romantic ones? She had to know what he had revealed to the minister.

"Does Norris think I'm having an affair?"

Wortham, plainly uncomfortable, cleared his throat several times before answering. "I don't feel I'm at liberty to divulge any more of our conversation, Vickie."

Frantic possibilities shot across her mind. The pastor was going to hang up before she could find out. What if Norris had revealed some link between her and Teddy—or what if he was troubled about Mrs. Mendel's sudden disappearance and had put two and two together—*What if, now when Norris disappears, Clark Wortham goes to the police?*

Without knowing exactly what she would say next, she blurted, "Reverend Wortham, I must see you—tonight!" She did have that extra truffle all prepared, after all.

He hesitated only an instant, but his voice sounded dutiful. "Very well. I'll be free after dinner, if you'd like to come by."

"No!" She took a deep breath and continued in a more controlled voice. "I have something to show you—at my apartment. I should have shown it to you the other night but, well, Norris burst in . . ."

She didn't know what else to say to convince him. "It will shed some light on all these peculiar happenings. And help me decide what to do."

"Do?"

"With the evidence."

His interest was obviously piqued. "Evidence?"

Well, she would think of something by the time he got there. "I have a few errands, but I should be home by eight. Can you drop by then? I'll only take a few minutes of your time."

Wortham agreed to come as she knew he would. Men were so transparent. He had been dying for an excuse to get her alone again, and she had offered him the perfect opportunity. Now all she had to do was keep him interested enough that he would stay for coffee. And a truffle. Then she would whisk him out and on his way before the nitro took effect. He would suffer a heart attack on the way home, most likely, *poor lamb*. Meantime, she'd flush the remaining truffles down the toilet and go to bed early.

She glanced at the clock: five-ten. No time to spare. As she pulled into traffic and headed for the hospital, she rang Norris' cell phone. He answered on the first ring.

"Where've you been?" She feigned irritation. "I've been trying to reach you for hours."

"I had chores to do," he said distantly.

The rat.

She said, "There's something very mysterious going on that I want to tell you about."

"Oh? What's that?"

"Not on the cell phone. Someone might hear. Maybe we can meet later."

"At your place?"

"No! Definitely not there! Someplace where we can't be overheard . . . . I know! How about City River Bridge, about seven? The traffic will have cleared out and we'll be in no danger from eavesdroppers."

He sounded dubious. "Aren't you being a bit melodramatic, Vickie?"

"When you hear what I have to tell you and see what I have to show you, then you can decide." She hung up abruptly, certain that he would come.

She pulled into the hospital parking lot and searched for a spot well away from the surveillance cameras. Not that her appearance carrying a tote bag of gifts should arouse suspicion. She congratulated herself on having wrapped the phony gift box. It was too bad that no one would ever know the full extent of her cleverness.

She grabbed the tote and hurried for the hospital's side entrance, the one reserved for hospital personnel. Once inside, she headed for the restroom, where she put on her reddish wig, her white nurse's shoes, and the name badge, covering all but one corner of the badge with the acrylic sweater. Glancing at her watch she congratulated herself on her timing: she still had ten minutes to locate Teddy's room.

She took out the truffle, carefully wrapped in wax paper, and concealed it loosely in the sweater pocket, taking care not to cradle it too closely and melt it with the warmth of her hand. As she hurried down the hall to the elevator, the remembrance of Teddy's outrageous message flashed across her mind: *How'd you like to spread 'em for me?* Or something like that. The nerve of Teddy Caplock, thinking he could entice her so easily.

As she stepped onto the elevator, unbidden rose the colorful images from the *Illustrated Kama Sutra*. Milch Cow, indeed! Under no circumstances would Teddy Caplock ever bend her over the copy machine, fling up her skirt, force his great glistening staub—

She was gripped by violent shudders as the elevator door opened. She realized that unconsciously she had been squeezing the truffle far too tightly. She forced herself to relinquish her hold and grasped the tote in both her trembling hands as she stepped off. She made her way to the nurses' station so as to glance quickly at room assignments before anyone questioned her presence. She found it immediately.

Caplock. Mere sight of the name brought a sudden moistness to her undergarment. It must be perspiration. Nervousness, perhaps. Nothing more.

24

At the far end of the corridor, the presence of a police guard lounging against the wall announced Teddy's whereabouts in Room 522, but it also presented Vickie with a fresh dilemma. She recognized him as being the same one who earlier had helped her search for the nonexistent bracelet at Teddy's bedside. Surely even with her disguise, he might recognize her.

Behind her, two kitchen attendants got off the service elevator pushing the supper cart and lumbered toward the nearest rooms, 501 and 502. Thankful for her prop, Vickie bent over the tote bag, pretending to rummage for something as she observed the arrangement of the trays on the cart. At first glance, locating Teddy's tray among so many would appear to be an impossible task. Fortunately, many would have been disposed of by the time they reached the other end of the hallway. Still, she needed to slip the truffle onto Teddy's plate before she was within recognition range of the guard.

The even-numbered room meals all appeared to be located on the right-hand side of the cart, so she must be careful, until the last moment, to stay behind the cart and to its left side, thus keeping the cart between her and the guard. Later she could remind the circle of witnesses, *"If a stranger had been in the hall, the guard surely would have noticed, wouldn't he?"*

One troubling aspect of the servers' conduct soon became apparent: The cart was never left unattended. The man on the even-numbered side stood by patiently while the woman on the opposite side delivered a meal to an odd-numbered room. So even if Vickie were to wait until the woman had left her side unattended, she might still be observed by the man on the odd-numbered side.

As always when her actions were condoned by the Almighty, a simple but ingenious plan occurred to her. But even as she congratulated herself on its brilliance, a crisp voice coming from directly behind her shattered her composure.

"You there! There's no visiting allowed on this wing during mealtimes."

Vickie turned to face a tall, commandingly solid nurse whose long-jawed sternness reminded her vaguely of her spinster Aunt Ned in Delaware, with whom she'd often been boarded while her parents went on church retreats. Aunt Ned, her mother's older sister, was even more strict and prudish than Vickie's parents, refusing to allow her to watch anything but Christian television channels and subjecting her small body to weekly purging with warm soapy enemas which the great woman administered with a certain undisguised relish.

Vickie lifted her chin and looked the nurse cold in the eye, the way she'd learned to do when she had lied to Aunt Ned. With a tinge of scorn, she said, "I'm not visiting. I'm from Admitting. The patient in—in Five-ten left this tote in Admitting, and I'm delivering it."

Aunt Ned's look-alike scowled icily. "There's been no new admission on this wing all day."

Vickie was up for the counter. Hadn't Aunt Ned challenged her repeatedly when Vickie would deny sneaking off to the creek bank to watch from the cover of bushes what the boys did to the girls under the bridge? Watch the boys begin by hanging by their knees from the steel supports, convincing the girls how much fun they were having, daring them to try it? Watch the boldest among the girls, who came often, Vickie soon learned, swing up onto a girder and hang upside down, skirt over her head, skimpy panties begging to be invaded? With horror and disgust, Vickie had seen one of the boys step up boldly and tug the panties to the girl's knees as she squealed in mock protest. Then, shouting threats of revenge, she swung upright and, holding to the bar by her hands, deftly kicked the underpants aside. She dropped to the ground, landing in a semi-crouch, yelling vows of retaliation, choosing as her prey the manliest boy. He broke into a half-hearted trot, not trying to escape her, and allowed her to tackle him to the ground and unzip his jeans. Then, leaping upon him, she straddled him and lunged up and down against him, up and down, up and down, up and down—

"I didn't go near the bridge!" Vickie blurted to the astonished nurse. Then she gulped and added, "The tote has been in Admissions for several days and no one knew who left it. It wasn't until I came back after being off work for several days that I identified it."

The nurse did not seem satisfied with this explanation, but stretched out a hand and said, "Just the same, only authorized personnel are allowed during mealtimes. Give me the tote; I'll take it to the patient."

"Oh but you see, that's why they sent me. I'm the only one who knows what the owner looks like." She forced her lips to spread in what she hoped would be taken for an ingenuous grin. "To tell the truth, I'd have been here sooner, but my first pick was the patient in Three-fifteen. But when I got there, I knew immediately I'd mixed two or three people up."

Before the nurse could protest, Vickie turned and hurried to catch up with the cart, calling over her shoulder. "I'll only be a minute . . . . Isn't that your pager?"

She didn't look back to see if Aunt Ned had taken the bait, but rushed to reach the cart, to resume the plan the nurse had interrupted. She approached the male attendant and peered quickly at his name badge: José Munoz. Then, waiting until the female server had left with a tray, she approached him. There was no time to spare.

"Anybody here named Munoz? There's a phone call for someone named José . . . ."

"I'm José Munoz," the man said. "But I don't know nobody that would call me."

The stupid oaf! Why didn't he just go?

"I think it's from the kitchen. Why don't you check at the nurses' station?" She spoke rapidly, with great authority. "I'll watch the cart. Go on! I don't have all day!"

He took off at a sprint while she hurriedly skirted the cart and, taking the slightly softened truffle from her pocket, dropped it onto the bread plate of tray 522. Too late, she spied a piece of sweater fuzz on the truffle's top, but there was no time to remove it. The other attendant was returning from her delivery.

Vickie smiled widely at her and said, "José's been called to the phone. They sent me to watch the cart till you got back. I'll be off now." Not waiting for an answer, she scurried to the nearby stairwell exit door and closed it quickly behind her. For a moment she leaned against it breathing hard, allowing the realization to sink in: Teddy Caplock would never assault her with sexual innuendos again, never sit on the edge of her desk and *tantalize—threaten her with that bulging—*

Over the years she had, on occasion, dreamed that it was she who swung from the bridge's rafters, sometimes having inadvertently forgotten to wear any panties at all. Always the dream involved a shadowy figure who would take advantage of her vulnerability and thrust his hands, or even his face, very near her forbidden parts. She would crash to the ground and wake with an abrupt start, sitting upright among tangled covers, sweating, shuddering, gasping for breath. Sometimes lately she would find herself muttering, "No you don't, Teddy Caplock!" without knowing why.

But no more. Teddy Caplock would soon be rotting in hell, with his own kind.

Meanwhile, there was still much work to do. That was merely one down, with three to go.

25

Before she left the Intermediate Care floor, Vickie could not resist opening the stairwell door just enough to peek out and observe the kitchen attendant deliver the correct tray to the guard outside room 522, home of Super Stud. Assured that she had done all she possible could to eliminate that loathsome sex monger, she hurried down one flight to Intensive Care, shucking off her nurse's disguise and stuffing it into the tote as she clattered down the concrete stairs.

She slipped into the hallway unobserved and headed for the nearest rest room. Ducking into the very end stall, she put on the black wig, the gaudy jewelry, the leopard spotted blouse, and awful stiletto street-walker heels. She got out her baggie of makeup and emerged to apply the dark lipstick and purple eye shadow before the mirror. The purple Roller Derby glasses completed the ensemble.

Still, she looked like Vickie Ledbetter. She would just have to keep her head down and work fast.

Her last act before leaving the rest room was to return to the stall and fill her syringe with nitroglycerine. This time there would be no slip-ups with the IV bag.

Luckily, Old Lady Mendel's room was several doors past the waiting room, enabling Vickie to check out the visitors. As before, Barbra Kline was seated far away from the others. It occurred to Vickie that by the regularity of her visits, Barbra was displaying uncommon devotion to an aunt she admittedly despised. There must be a tidy inheritance involved. If so, the old woman concealed her wealth well.

Vickie grinned to herself with the realization that, if Mrs. Mendel's death were by some remote chance ruled murder, Barbra would naturally be found guilty and would be denied the inheritance. *Perfect.*

At was nearly a half hour until visiting time. She sauntered toward Sylvia Mendel's room, pretending to be looking for the rest room, waiting for the corridor to clear of hospital personnel. Finally, when she saw her chance, she darted into the room. In the light of the bleeping monitor, she recognized the old hag, sleeping peacefully. There was no mistaking her identity: the special aroma that was Sylvia Mendel hung in the air. It was enough to make a person gag.

In four long strides, Vickie reached the bedside, drew out the syringe and plunged it into the IV bag. As the last of the thick solution emptied out of the syringe, the door flew open and a tall, fiery-eyed male nurse stormed in. But Vickie's reflexes were sure, and she jerked the syringe out the moment of the hinges' first creak. However, she did it with such force that she tore the bag slightly, well above the liquid level. The bag would be safe, if only the nurse didn't see the tear, fear contamination and change it out.

The nurse's booming voice could have been heard all the way to the nurses' station. "Who gave you permission to come in here?"

Vickie hardly dared speak, knowing she couldn't possibly sound like Barbra Kline. She dared not glance back at the bag, or the incredibly well-developed nurse's gaze might follow hers. As yet he hadn't taken his eyes off Vickie. Dear God, was the man pursuing her, even while she wore this ridiculous gaudy outfit? Was there no way she could conceal her magnetic appeal?

Then she must let it work to her advantage. It was time to divert him by turning on the charm. She quickly dropped the syringe into the tote—taking care not to stick herself this time—and sashayed past him toward the door, saying in a sultry whisper, "I guess I looked at my watch wrong."

His dark-fringed eyes followed her, widening in wonder. She was obviously getting to him. He cleared his throat and said, "Uh Miss, I may be out of line, but—"

She turned and batted her purple lids, giving him her most seductive look and pitching her voice an octave lower. "Yesss?"

He went on hesitantly. "I think I know a surgeon who could help you with that hip displacement problem."

Jerk! She couldn't think of a retort, so she wheeled around and stomped out. *Men!* They were all alike! They all thought they were irresistible, and they all had the same thing on their minds. This klutz didn't fool her for a minute.

She hurried back to the stairwell door, not even bothering to check to see if she was observed before entering it. Her watch told her that she was on target. There was plenty of time to get home and prepare a trap for the good pastor before her rendezvous with that dweeb Norris.

On the ground floor, she had the presence of mind to peer out cautiously before she exited. Or maybe the fates were just with her again. Because standing only ten feet away was a police officer, and the first words she heard him say were "Teddy Caplock."

She sucked in her breath and backed out of sight, but kept the door slightly ajar so she could hear. The policeman seemed to be talking to another man, possibly another officer, and he was obviously asking directions to Teddy's room. Her spirits soared: the nitro had already done its work, and Teddy had bought the farm, eaten the melon, kicked the bucket, sank to the drain, fallen into the blow-hole.

But no one would have a clue how he really died; it was a heart attack, pure and simple. She was safe. Her chastity was safe. The world was rid of one more prick. Perhaps later she would experience the elation she had presumed she would feel at this moment. It probably just hadn't caught up with her yet.

Now if Sylvia Mendel would only be equally obliging, then she would feel elated.

To her horror, the officer elected to take the stairs, and the door swung open in her face. Without thinking, Vickie gasped and cried out, "I didn't do it!"

Startled, the officer stared for a minute, then grinned, stepped back, and held the door open for her. "I get that a lot," he said. "But usually not from a pretty lady." He was, she decided, trying to entrap her with his rugged good looks and his hard, hard body.

She slithered by, feeling the heat pass between them. He wanted her, was even now undressing her with his agate black eyes. His after shave—with a hint of musk—had been deliberately applied as an aphrodisiac. Perhaps he had seen her around the hospital before and had cleverly managed this so-called chance encounter. How, she was not sure; she only knew that a sexually craven man could hatch diabolical schemes to get what he wanted.

It was an effort not to turn and give him a withering glare, but she must keep focused. She walked deliberately to the ground floor rest room, removed her Barbra Kline disguise, and prepared to leave the building as Vickie Ledbetter. As she walked out, she threw a casual glance around the

area, but the hard-bodied cop was nowhere to be seen. The woman at the
Information desk smiled in recognition.

"So your friend has gone home?" she said.

"What?" Vickie was not even sure she was talking to her.

"I notice you're taking your gifts home with you," the woman said.

Vickie glanced down at the tote. She had meant to discard the fake
gift in the rest room trash. "Uh—yes. My friend isn't here any more." She
couldn't help adding, "He died."

Without waiting for condolences, she rushed out, pretending to be
in tears. Once back in her car, she pondered how to dispose of the toteful
of evidence that would tie her to the murders. Strange that she hadn't
planned this ahead of time. Peculiar that she had neglected to factor in the
extra drive across town to deposit a different item into a dozen different
dumpsters. It was almost as if some perverse part of her had wanted to get
caught, if for no better reason than so everyone would at last realize how
clever she was.

But no, she would manage. It was only a little after six. She could still
drive across town and back, go home and prepare for the pastor, make
her appointment with Norris, and be back home by eight o'clock to greet
Clark Wortham. It would work out. She was in the right, after all, and
Right Wills Out. Surely God would condone her heroic efforts to rid the
world of this sexual evil, even at the risk of her own safety.

With a great sense of accomplishment, she drove toward the freeway
that would take her on her cross-town mission. Her target was an area of
low-income apartment complexes with easily accessible trash receptacles.
Since the trip was unavoidable, she endeavored to spend it wisely,
meticulously planning her next moves, moves that would eliminate the last
two accomplices to this long reign of sin.

26

With unrelenting regularity, the dashboard clock counted off precious minutes while Vickie rushed from dumpster to dumpster, endowing each with a perfectly good item of apparel. The fate of each was imbued with a last minute element of importance, like that of an unloved child at the moment of sending him out into the world to make his own way.

The least deserving, leopard-print blouse was the first to go, sailing high, settling slowly, draping itself prettily over a used Pamper or two in the far corner of the first receptacle. In the next, the acrylic sweater landed in an unidentifiable pottage that almost at once seeped brownish-red into the recalcitrant threads of one sleeve. The gold earrings and bangles clunked inelegantly against discarded cans like tin upon tin, and the purple roller derby glasses nestled fondly among the contents of a steaming bag of yard clippings already beginning to compost. The starkly tacky stiletto-heeled shoes sank to an ignoble end among a stack of badly mutilated Quayle for President placards.

Finally, the syringes found a home among others of their kind, she suspected, in an alley behind a local drug rehab center. She took great pleasure in topping that offering with the bogus gift package, placed tantalizingly within reach of the first rummager, who would be sure he had found a treasure.

And then she felt cleansed, pure and virginal again, chaste and pious, a woman who could look the world in the eye with an unblemished conscience. Only, like all true altruists, the world could never know of her beneficence. If she boasted of it, the precious element of altruism would be lost.

Once the evidence was trashed, she turned toward her apartment, avoiding the temptation to speed for fear of being pulled over and ticketed. No need to push herself, anyhow; her cause was just, and time would be provided for all things to be accomplished. Even now, from the heights of the waning afternoon sky, an Elysian chorus was no doubt pealing hosannas. And although she deserved them, she felt some acknowledgment was in order, so borrowing from that frequently appearing saint, she breathed, *Thank yew. Thank yew ver' much.*

She sailed into her building and rode up to her floor unobserved. It was her day. Nothing could deter her.

The time was seven o'clock. She would need no more than fifteen minutes to set a trap for the clergyman and change into a dark, inconspicuous outfit. The drive to City River Bridge should take no more than ten minutes. She could easily make her seven-thirty appointment with Norris and be home to catch her breath and change clothes again before Clark arrived.

She had carefully preserved the extra truffle and now knew how it should be presented to the good pastor. With meticulous care, she would stack the chocolates in an artful pyramid, so that it would be impossible to take any but the top one. She had a small crystal saucer that would suffice for the eleven pieces that were left. There was even a package of paper doilies in her cabinet, the perfect touch of elegance for the discerning hostess.

She arranged five truffles on the doily-covered saucer, then balanced five more, bridging the spaces between the bottom row, and topping these with her magic bullet, slightly but perhaps not noticeably shop-worn from its trip to the hospital and back. There was no way Clark Wortham could select one of the other pieces without toppling the entire pyramid. The top piece might just as well have his name on it.

But what if he refused to take one at all?

While she pondered this revolting possibility, she changed into a black turtleneck and jeans. Then she filled the coffee maker and set it to begin in forty minutes. That should give her an ample interval to send Norris on the first leg of his trip to the Gulf of Mexico, get home, slip into something frilly, and pour the coffee into her best china cups before receiving the holy visitor with the horny mind.

Oh, he would take the candy, all right; she could pout, she could flirt, she could do whatever it took. If he refused, she would cry, if necessary, and if that failed, she would force it on him, if she had to hold him at knife-point. No man of the cloth was going to screw up her plans.

She smirked at the thought: Clark Wortham was not going to screw anything. Or anyone. Ever.

There was a time when she had almost dreamed of sleeping with a preacher, once very long ago. No, that was not entirely accurate, now that she thought about it. She could not allow herself to fantasize about the charismatic visiting evangelist with the blow-dried coif and the sun-bronzed face and the wide-lapelled suit with the tight, tight trousers—could not condone in herself the feeling of helpless submission when, during his sermon, he turned pewter-grey eyes full upon her and raked her clothes from her body with his gaze.

After the impassioned invitational hymn that night, she had stumbled home limp and in a swivety daze, had quickly fallen into a fevered sleep, and had dreamed—not of the volatile preacher, but—of Jesus. Yes, she had read of nuns becoming the bride of Christ, and now she knew what it meant. It seemed more acceptable to be touched by the wand of the Lamb than by that of his very earthy disciple. It was a night of ecstasy about which she felt no shame. After all, who can question communing with the Lord?

Often, before and since, she had dreamed of near-encounters with appropriately chaste partners, but she always woke with a start of alarm before the consummating act. The dreams, she knew, were the work of the Devil. The sudden awakenings were by the grace of God.

If things had been different, she might have entertained Clark Wortham's advances, might have accepted his attentions and even, eventually, an engagement ring. She would of course make the perfect vicar's wife: naturally modest and retiring, honed in the uxorial skills. Perhaps, when the new rector arrived to fill the vacancy occasioned by Clark Wortham's demise, she would consider the idea of his courtship.

Unless, of course, he were already married. Then she would weigh the feasibility of serving the newcomer's wife one of her famous truffles. By that time, she should have her technique perfected.

The heavenly paean in her honor continued as she emerged from her apartment and blended into the gathering twilight in her dark clothing. Passersby were obviously entirely too insensitive to hear the music, or if they heard, would have no clue that it was meant for her. Still, she lifted her chin and mumbled, "Thank yew. Thank yew ver' much."

Traffic toward the city's outskirts was surprisingly sluggish, something she hadn't counted on. Eventually she spotted the problem ahead: a rear-end collision in the right lane, police cars and wreckers clogging the area, lights flashing, rubber-neckers slowing to a crawl. Vickie tried to edge left, along with those in front of and behind her. For long minutes at a time there was no forward movement at all. Perspiration caused her hands to feel slippery on the wheel. Repeatedly she glanced at the dashboard clock, willing it to stand still.

Seven-thirty came and went. Once past the wreck, traffic sped up and dispersed, but she was still several miles from the bridge. Would Norris wait for her? Damn him, why did he refuse to have a cell phone?

It occurred to her that perhaps Norris had also been caught in the snare and would understand her tardiness. But until she pulled up to bridge's approach and parked, the fact that she would actually arrive ahead of him hadn't dawned on her. It was seven-forty. Where in God's name was he? It was just like Norris Griswold to be late for his own funeral.

She got out of the car and strolled toward the deserted bridge. Dusk was fast descending. The sky off in the distance, away from the city's spectral monoliths, was orange, pink, purple. The river looked ominously dark. Deep shadows charcoaled the torpid water, and lights from the far shore shimmered on its surface like a film of oil, buoyed along on an invisible, turgid undercurrent toward the ocean. She imagined Norris floating face down, his gently waffling body wafting southward, frenzied fish nipping at his nose, his lolling tongue, his still-surprised bug-eyes, the ends of the ever-present necktie. A snapping turtle attaching itself to the cuff of his trousers, perhaps, or even to the featureless indifference of his lifeless crotch—nothing new there.

And the whole flotilla of bloating carcass, barnacled but disappointed amphibian, and orbiting river perch whittling away greedily at their newfound din-dins, would wend its meandering course out of her life, accompanied by a rousing chorus of—what? Onward, Christian Soldiers, perhaps. She wondered if her chorale took requests.

Leaning against the rail, she relaxed, willing herself to be like the current, going with the flow, taking events as they came. She couldn't worry that Norris was late to his own spectacular dive, which meant that Clark Wortham would be left waiting at her doorstep for his heart attack. All would be accomplished in due time, tonight. That much was certain.

Perhaps she should phone Clark, put him off for a half-hour, even though she detested last-minute alterations in plans. But as she turned back toward her car, the headlights of an oncoming vehicle temporarily blinded her. With relief, she saw it veer off and come to a stop beside her car. Thank God. It must be almost eight o'clock. Her victims were queuing up.

As Norris emerged, the shadowy outline of a suit coat offered assurance that he would go out in style. She hoped to God he was wearing that awful yellow necktie with the blue dots. Maybe a week in the river would improve its appearance. Providing he didn't sink to the bottom and remain unfound. In which case, a shark in the Gulf might end up gobbling Norris's neckwear—and bits of its owner as well, what the river perch left behind after their feeding frenzy was spent.

Norris Griswold—how had she borne him all this time? Why had she suffered the interminable evenings on their so-called "dates", dining on cafeteria fare, choking down bland fish and featureless vegetables, underbaked rolls and ice-box pie that tasted of refrigerator coils, all so the tightwad wouldn't be obliged to leave a tip? And for what? For him to dive among her melons at the first opportunity, like the crazed lecher she'd always suspected him to be!

And that dreadful pornographic movie—what was that all about? What had he expected to gain? It was his feeble, inept attempt to seduce her, without doubt. But she was much too savvy for that transparent approach. Did he take her for a complete sniveling twit?

And yet, even now, the sight of that lascivious Act, performed so wantonly by two sweating creatures who obviously enjoyed their so-called work, projected forty times larger than life in Cinema-Color, their gasps and groans of ecstasy magnified by Surround-Sound—even now it haunted her dreams. She couldn't get away from the image, not even when, panting for breath, she sprang from the covers and threw herself onto her knees at her bedside, commanding Satan to desist. It never worked. The more she tried to forget, the brighter the image, the more vivid the features, until their resemblance to her and—who?—Teddy Caplock?—became undeniable.

Did Norris hope to seduce her by showing her Vickie making jig-jig with Teddy Caplock, for God's sake? Now, as he stood before her in the bridge's gloom, stooped and needy, she wanted to shake him until he made the dreadful apparition go away. But he never would. Norris was too dense to understand what he had done.

That petulant whine that was uniquely Norris's caught at her jawbone, setting her teeth on edge. "This had better be important. I almost got killed getting here. Some jerk almost sideswiped me trying to get around that collision. Tried to edge me right off the road into a ditch."

Pity he didn't succeed. It would've saved me from having to dirty my hands.

She looked down at her upturned palms and for the first time doubted her ability to pull it off. Norris seemed larger than she'd realized. This feat would take more strength than she possessed. She would have to depend on leverage. Hit him high, catch him off balance.

The trick would be to entice him to lean over the rail. She affected a level of excitement that she hardly had to fake. She pointed down at the base of the bridge. "You have to see this! I don't know what to make of it!"

"What?" he said, obviously intrigued, or as intrigued as that muffle-head ever got.

"See for yourself!" She caught his arm and dragged him toward the rail.

But leverage depended on getting a running start. She dropped his arm and pushed him forward. "Go on. Lean over. Look down at the pilings. Tell me what it looks like to you."

Hesitantly, he stepped to the rail and bent forward. "It's too dark down there. What am I supposed to be looking for?"

She backed to the opposite rail to give herself as much distance as possible to build up momentum.

"Keep looking," she called. "Your eyes will adjust in a minute." She pushed off and gave it everything she had.

That noise—what was the noise? A cell phone? Her phone! Clark Wortham must be at her door—

Norris straightened and turned toward the sound. "Is that your cell phone ringing?"

She was flying toward him.

Flying. Norris stepped aside. *Can't stop!*

Oh no—

27

Still glowing from the impromptu accolades of the chief for his speedy resolution of the recent spate of violent deaths and near-deaths, Roscoe pulled up in front of Vickie's apartment, parked behind another squad car, and turned to Sonja, who sat beside him. "I have to check on Lambert and Carmelo. I won't be long."

Sonja caught his arm, gouging those red talons into the sleeve of his uniform, and answering in a gravelly growl. "Oh no. You're not leaving me out here with a murderer running loose! I'm coming with you."

She got out and followed him up the walk. Actually, he was flattered that she wanted to be with him. Now she would see him in action, watch him wrap a very complicated case.

He held open the door for her and said, "You don't have to be afraid. Yes, a murderer is out there, but not for long. Not after today." He pushed the elevator button and looked back toward the manager's apartment as he heard a slight sound. Reuther, who was peering out at them through a small crack, hurriedly retreated and closed his door.

When the elevator opened, a thin slightly shabby cleric stepped off and, as he passed them, Sonja whispered, "That's Vickie's minister."

The preacher apparently heard her and wheeled around. "Officer? I'm Clark Wortham. I understand from my housekeeper, Mrs. Twickham, that you came by my house looking for me."

This was untidy. Roscoe preferred to choose the time and place for interviews. With the scowl of a Busy Man, he pulled out his notebook and checked his data. "Uh-yeah. Vickie Ledbetter's caller I.D. shows that you phoned her from your cell phone at eight-oh-seven Wednesday night."

He expected Wortham to be surprised at his quick detection. But the preacher said without hesitation, "That's right. She had asked me to drop by at eight, said it was urgent. But when I got here, she didn't answer. So I called her."

"From the hallway? You knew her number from memory?"

"Well-first I had to phone Mrs. Twickham and have her look up the number. Then I called." He paused, a little too eager to get all the facts straight. "I knew Vickie must be inside, you see, because she said she was having company for dinner, but it was urgent that I see her after they left."

"Company, you say? Who? Norris Griswold?"

"No, I'm certain it wasn't Norris. I don't know who it was."

"Did she tell you what was so urgent?"

The minister hesitated, the slack, sallow lines of his face drawn down in concentration. "She—thought Norris Griswold was unbalanced. She thought he might try to kill—"

Sonja broke in with a laugh. "Norris? Kill?"

Roscoe frowned at her interruption, but she wasn't looking at him. He said, "Looks are deceiving."

"—kill himself," Wortham finished. Lamely. He looked from one to the other, as if anxious for withheld validation.

Despite Roscoe's best attempt at keeping a noncommittal demeanor, the corner of his mouth twitched at the irony. He said, "When was the last time you saw Vickie Ledbetter?"

"The night before, here at her apartment," Wortham said, wan cheeks coloring slightly, pale fringed eyelids batting rapidly behind the wire frames. "Griswold broke in on us. It was innocent enough, but Norris misunderstood. The next afternoon he came to see me. He thought I was romantically interested in her." He stopped, stammering, reaching into his breast pocket for a handkerchief. "I-I've said too much. I'm violating a confidence."

Roscoe flipped his notebook closed, enormously satisfied, marveling once again at the ease with which he could intimidate the hell out of even a man of the cloth. "That's okay, padre. I think we have enough for now."

He pushed the elevator button again and ushered Sonja inside, then turned to Wortham. "We'll get a formal statement later. You'll be around." It wasn't a question.

"Of course," the minister said, his mouth still agape with words left unsaid as the doors closed.

As Roscoe and Sonja rode to the third floor, she moved closer to him and murmured, "I still can't believe it."

He shrugged, affecting nonchalance for her benefit. "Lotsa surprises in this business, but you get used to 'em. Some guys at the station were completely thrown by this one. But I had it figured. I could've almost predicted it." He smiled secretly, again recalling the chief's praise of his uncanny detective work.

"Oh yeah?" There was more than a hint of sarcasm in Sonja's tone as they stepped off into Vickie's hallway.

He felt his blood rise with indignation. Women! Always quick with the subtle put-down shot from the hip. *Okay, sister.* He didn't usually discuss cases in progress, but this one was pretty well wrapped. Maybe he'd make her eat that jibe, dazzle her with just exactly how he figured the whole thing out with such ease.

The door to Vickie's apartment was ajar. As they entered, Sergeant Carmelo, coming from the bedroom, nodded toward him and said, "Nothing in here. Like you figured."

Lambert stuck his head out from the kitchenette. "Here either. The place is clean. Except for this." He came in holding up a paper sack.

Roscoe leaned over and peered into it, then took out a bottle. "All this is the old woman's medicine? From next door."

Sonja said, "What's Vickie doing with it?"

Lambert said, "The super, Reuther, let the Ledbetter woman into the Mendel apartment to get it. She said the old lady asked her to bring it to the hospital."

Roscoe dropped the bottle back into the bag. "Guess she won't be needing it now."

Sonja said, "Poor old soul. Do you know how it happened?"

He allowed his smugness to show. "Oh sure. Hers was the easiest to solve." He didn't add that old lady Mendel had given them the best clue. The only niggling regret was that they didn't pay attention to her when she first talked about being suffocated. Then she might not be where she was today.

"So who did it?" Sonja asked.

He weighed the probability that Sonja would brag about all this at the office and decided, at this point, it didn't matter. "I guess it won't hurt to tell you. They've probably already picked her up by now."

"Mrs. Mendel's niece?"

Roscoe snorted at her naiveté. "An amateur's supposition. It's seldom the obvious one. I knew right away Barbra Kline didn't do it. It wasn't her style."

He led Sonja over to the living room sofa and sat beside her. "Mrs. Mendel showed up at Dr. Jacob's office before it was even open one morning. The office nurse complained that she'd received an abusive, threatening call that Jacobs would get hit by a law suit if she didn't let the old woman come right away. I guess the nurse just lost it. As soon as they were alone, she tried to suffocate the old broad. Later, when she saw that she hadn't succeeded, she claimed she was giving her CPR to bring her around."

Sonja asked, "Then why didn't you arrest her right away?"

"Mrs. Mendel would've had to file charges at that point. Anyway, when she finally came around enough to be interviewed, she kept insisting it wasn't the nurse that tried to kill her. But her brain was so addled, she couldn't think of the name of the woman who did it. Or maybe she was just pretending."

"Why would she do that? Fear?"

Roscoe nodded. "It wouldn't be the first time. But apparently once Jacob's office nurse got wind of the fact that Mendel was going to finger her, she was only too willing to provide the nitro to the would-be murderer."

"Wait. Back up. You're saying Dr. Jacob's nurse was only an accessory? For who, then?"

"Art Reuther, the apartment manager. In drag." Before she could protest, he hurried on. "I know it sounds far-fetched to a novice, but we don't make accusations without proof."

Sonja frowned. "Like what?"

"Well, for one thing, Reuther's phone records show he called Jacob's office nurse the day of old lady Mendel's first attack. Why would he do that except to blackmail her? Somehow he figured out what she'd done to the old broad and decided to use his knowledge to his advantage."

"Which was?"

"To get her to supply him with a lethal dose of something to finish the job."

"But why? What did the apartment super have against poor old Mrs. Mendel?" Sonja said.

"It wasn't her, exactly; it was her dog. She'd been keeping a pet against apartment restrictions. The mutt had crapped all over the place, so Reuther tossed him out. Some kid took him home, and when his mom found out the pooch had just been thrown out the door, she called the Humane Society. They were giving Reuther a hard time about animal cruelty, and he just blew his stack. Simple as that."

When she opened her mouth to voice some insipid bit of female skepticism, he jumped in to cut her off. "Anyhow, we've got an eye witness. A male nurse. He saw the whole thing."

"Which was what?"

"He saw a person wearing a wig fiddling with the old lady's IV bag. Later he figured out the person was doctoring it."

"A person wearing a wig? Or a man?"

Roscoe shifted uncomfortably, remembering the male nurse's vague-off-handed description, but he stood his ground. "Apparently you didn't catch what I said. It was a male nurse."

"So?" Sonja raised her eyebrows in skepticism.

Lord help us, women were simple-minded. "Don't you know that, as far as gay guys go—and male nurses are always gay—all men look like women. They can't tell the difference."

After he had let this soak in, he added. "But this one'll recognize Reuther in a line-up once we slap a wig on 'im."

Sonja rolled her mascara clumps ceilingward and shook her head, as if there was a flaw in his logic. Then she was back chewing on his tail like a junk-yard dog. "So why did you say Mrs. Mendel won't be needing her medicine now?"

"Because it just so happened that the extra nitro was exactly what the old girl needed to pull her through, only her doctor never would've prescribed such a big dose for such a small-framed woman. With any luck, she'll eventually come back home fit as ever, ready to hector that bitchy niece of hers for another twenty years."

Lambert had been talking on his cell phone. He stepped up and said, "That was Frances at the station. Gary's able to have visitors now. Somebody ought to stand by him."

Roscoe sighed heavily, remembering what a good officer Gary had been. He gave Sonja's hand a quick squeeze. "I've gotta follow up on this one. If it weren't for me, Gary would still be a respected police officer."

"How so?"

"If I hadn't insisted on a bodyguard for Teddy, Gary wouldn't have been on duty outside Teddy's room that evening."

Sonja looked puzzled. "But I thought Gary just had a heart attack."

"So did we, at first. He might've died, if he'd been anywhere else. Luckily a doctor was passing by and issued a Code Blue. It was the doctor who first suspected that somebody had slipped Gary a big dose of nitroglycerine and induced the attack. So it didn't take an Einstein to figure out who."

She waited expectantly. "Well?"

Roscoe hesitated. If he said nothing—ever—he wouldn't betray a friend. But the proud tradition in his family of law enforcers, which ran back three generations, would not allow him to keep silent. From his father and grandfather he had inherited his uncanny ability to ferret out a criminal instinctively.

He summoned all his resolve and said, "It was Teddy."

"Teddy?" she said incredulously. Then she grinned and playfully slapped his shoulder. "Get out! How could that basket case do it—and why?"

"There's no doubt about it. They pumped Gary's stomach and found blanket fuzz. Had to be from Teddy's blanket. He must've been hiding the dose under the covers until the right time."

She leaned back and crossed her arms across her chest, drumming her foot irritably against the leg of the coffee table. "That makes no sense whatsoever."

It was the kind of stupid reaction he'd learn to expect from her. So he didn't mind setting her straight. "It was a supposed suicide pact. Only Teddy never got to go through with his part."

"Suicide? But why?"

"The two were secretly lovers."

Sonja snorted. "Teddy and Gary? Come on! Since when?"

"It must've started soon after Gary was assigned to guard Teddy. It must've been an instantaneous thing, because when Vickie came up to look for her bracelet, Teddy misunderstood and thought she was coming to see Gary, and he had such a violent fit when she left that he tried to pull out his IV. You don't do that unless there's a lot of emotion involved."

Sonja was silent, trying to take it all in. He detested the doubt written all over her face. She said, "I don't know how you get a suicide pact out of that. Or a love affair, either, for that matter."

That was the trouble with dealing with non-professionals. They lack skills in deduction. He leaned over and tapped her forehead. "Think. Pulling out his IV was an act of suicide, right? Luckily, Gary was on hand to call the nurse. But it made him realize how much he meant to Teddy. And how he felt about Teddy in return."

"How do you know?"

"Because soon after that he told me—'Man,' he said, 'if I'da let Caplock croak, I'da really had my tail in a crack!' Now surely, as innocent as you are, even you know that there's no way to misinterpret what that means."

Sonja stared at him, then guffawed like a common bar maid. "You letch! Not everything anybody says has a sexual connotation."

"This did," he insisted. "It was only a matter of elemental deduction to figure out that, after that, Gary made a pact that if ever Teddy tried to commit suicide again, Gary would follow suit."

He was warming to his theory, but paused to let dim-witted Sonja catch up to him. She still didn't look convinced. In fact, one hand held the corners of her mouth as if she were trying to keep from laughing. There was nothing to do but go on.

"Teddy was really agitated after that incident. Every time I visited, he was obviously edgy. He seemed to be trying to tell me something, if only he could talk. Gradually I figured out that he must want me to replace Gary with someone else. My theory is that he was jealous, afraid Vickie might keep coming back and hit on Gary. She did come back, you know. I saw her in the waiting room. She tried to pretend she was there to visit somebody else, but later I scoped it out that she was just trying to put the make on Gary."

Sylvia sniffed. "I have a hard time imagining Vickie putting the make on anybody."

"I should've replaced Gary when I first suspected, but I just hadn't gotten around to it yet. So Teddy decided to take things into his own hands."

"Oh? How?" Her curiosity was obviously aroused.

"He lapsed into a fake coma."

"Fake? But didn't you tell me the doctor warned that he might lapse back into unconsciousness from time to time?"

Sonja was right. He had almost forgotten. "Yes," he said slowly. Then he brightened. "But it didn't matter. Gary thought Teddy'd bought it—so he took the nitro that Teddy had been saving in his blanket, and Gary fulfilled his end of the pact. Then Teddy pulled a gotcha and came around."

He sighed in relief. "Legally, Teddy can't be charged for tricking Gary."

"Couldn't Teddy have been in a real coma?"

"That's what I'd like to believe. That it wasn't a trick, just a coincidence. That's the report I've filed. Nobody can prove otherwise. And at least, when Teddy recovers, he and Gary will still have a relationship." It was the least he could do for his old AC-DC friend.

"Wow," Sonja said. "That's some detective work."

Roscoe shrugged deprecatingly. "What can I say? I'm a professional. It's what I do."

He settled back and went on. "But the case of Vickie Ledbetter was my greatest challenge. Everyone else thought Norris pushed her off that bridge. All the evidence pointed to it. But from the beginning, I knew that explanation was too simple."

"So how did you figure out what really happened?"

Roscoe started to say it was elemental, but that would belittle his powers of deduction. Not every officer, no matter how well trained, could have cracked this case and done it so quickly. "That story of Pastor Wortham's doesn't hold water. By his own admission, he and Vickie were together the night before. Norris Griswold even admits breaking in on them."

He paused ominously. "Norris said Vickie wasn't wearing any shoes that night. She was bare footed."

"Oh whoopee," Sonja said, baring her teeth in a full-lipped smirk. "Was she having sex with her toes?"

But Sonja didn't know how far ahead of the game he had been, didn't know he had spent the morning building a case, even interviewing parishioners.

"It might interest you to know that at the last church supper, Vickie suddenly disappeared just as the musical program began. Later one of the church women found an article of clothing belonging to Vickie. It was under the table!"

"So? What does that mean?"

"Don't you get it? Do I have to draw you a picture? While the musicians performed, Vickie and Wortham were under the table gettin' it on!"

"Well I'll be—So Clark Wortham and Norris Griswold were jealous rivals."

"Well, in Wortham's eyes, they were. That's why he followed Vickie to her tryst with Norris on the bridge, intending to push Norris off. But he missed and pushed Vickie off by accident."

"But if that's so, why wouldn't Norris tell you?"

Roscoe grinned triumphantly. It was the small nuances of a case that tested a man's mettle. "Here's where the real detective work came in. Remember I said in Wortham's eyes they were rivals?"

"Yes . . ."

"In Norris's eyes, he and Vickie were rivals for Wortham's affection."

"Double wow!" Sonja's kohl-fringed eyes shone with admiration. At times like this she was downright pretty.

He extended his long legs underneath the coffee table, ready for the home stretch. "Norris is secretly in love with Wortham. But it's hardly a secret. He admits to being enraged when Wortham came over to return the article of clothing Vickie left at the church supper. And he admits to being devastated when he found Wortham and a bare-footed Vickie together in this apartment. He also admits going to see Wortham the day of the bridge tryst."

Sonja said, "So when Wortham accidentally pushed Vickie off the bridge—"

"Norris covered for him. Out of love."

"But what first made you suspect Wortham?"

Roscoe narrowed his eyes and fixed her with a stern gaze for emphasis. "Always remember this, Sonja: When you see someone who seems too goody-good, suspect him. A repressed man is a potentially dangerous man. The caged animal is always violent. It's one of the cardinal principles of police work. Forget it at your peril."

Sonja took it all in, then sighed and shook her head sadly. "All this tragedy makes me so sorry for my part in sending those silly e-mail messages to poor Vickie."

Roscoe dismissed it. "An office prank. Surely Vickie could take a joke."

"It wasn't what we did," Sonja said. "It was the spirit behind it. We girls thought Vickie was so straight-laced that a little dirty talk would freak her out. We used to gather around the coffee machine in the mornings because from there we could watch her reaction when she read our messages. Even some of the guys were in on it."

Roscoe rose to go, pulling her to her feet as well. "Believe me. I know human nature. Those messages didn't bother Vickie. So forget about it."

As she passed in front of him, she gave his chest an affectionate pat. "You're so smart, Roscoe. Is there anything you don't know?"

"Not much, babe," he said. "But it's taken me years to get to this point. I've put in a helluva lot of legwork over the years to hone these instincts for detection. Experience: that's what turns a raw rooky from the East Side into a skillful professional."

At last she seemed genuinely convinced, although she'd been an even harder sell than the chief. With a smile that carved her cheeks with deep dimpled commas, she reached over and picked up a crystal saucer of truffles from the coffee table and held them toward him. "After all your work, you deserve a treat. Here. Have a chocolate. Vickie won't be needing them now."

"Thanks," he said, picking the top candy. "Believe I will."

Get Published, Inc!
Thorofare, NJ 08086
03 September 2009
BA2009246